THUNDER OVER THE
SUPERSTITIONS

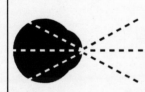

This Large Print Book carries the
Seal of Approval of N.A.V.H.

THUNDER OVER THE SUPERSTITIONS

ROGUE LAWMAN:
A GIDEON HAWK WESTERN

PETER BRANDVOLD

Including a bonus story featuring the Rio Concho Kid:
Blood and Lust in Old Mexico

THORNDIKE PRESS
A part of Gale, Cengage Learning

GALE
CENGAGE Learning·

Farmington Hills, Mich • San Francisco • New York • Waterville, Maine
Meriden, Conn • Mason, Ohio • Chicago

GALE
CENGAGE Learning·

LIBRARY OF CONGRESS CATALOGING-IN-PUBLICATION DATA

Names: Brandvold, Peter, author.
Title: Thunder over the superstitions : rogue lawman : a Gideon Hawk western /
by Peter Brandvold.
Description: Large print edition. | Waterville, Maine : Thorndike Press, 2016. | ©
2015 | Series: Thorndike Press large print western | "Including a bonus story
featuring the Rio Concho Kid: Blood and Lust in Old Mexico."
Identifiers: LCCN 2015041182 | ISBN 9781410487155 (hardcover) | ISBN 1410487156
(hardcover)
Subjects: LCSH: Large type books. | GSAFD: Western stories.
Classification: LCC PS3552.R3236 T46 2016 | DDC 813/.54—dc23
LC record available at http://lccn.loc.gov/2015041182

Published in 2016 by arrangement with Peter Brandvold

Printed in Mexico
1 2 3 4 5 6 7 20 19 18 17 16

For who else but
James and Livia Reasoner

CONTENTS

Chapter 1
The Laughing Lady

The rogue lawman, Gideon Hawk, smelled blood on the howling wind.

Beneath the wind, he heard the pattering of an off-key piano. The music, if you could call it that, emanated from somewhere ahead in the dusty, wind-battered desert settlement on the outskirts of which he halted his grulla.

A weathered sign along the road announced SPOTTED HORSE, ARIZ. TERR.

Hawk slid his big, silver-plated Russian Model Smith & Wesson .44 from its holster positioned for the cross draw on his left hip. He flipped the latch on the top-break revolver with his gloved thumb, breaking it open. He filled the cylinder's one empty chamber with a bullet from his shell belt, then snapped the gun closed.

He returned the pistol to its holster and filled the empty chamber in his horn-gripped Colt, which occupied the holster on his right hip, strapped around his waist by a second shell belt. He returned that gun, too, to its holster but did not snap the keeper thong home across the hammer. He let the straps dangle freely, both pistols ready to be drawn.

Hawk had followed a killer here. A killer carrying one of Hawk's own bullets in his hide. It was the killer's blood that Hawk smelled on the wind. The piano's pattering did not sound like a funeral dirge, but it might as well have been, because Hawk intended for the music, if you could call it that, to be the last notes his quarry ever heard.

He loosened his Henry repeater in the scabbard strapped to his saddle, the walnut stock with brass butt plate jutting up above his right stirrup fender. Then he nudged the horse ahead down the broad street. Shabby, false-fronted buildings loomed to both sides, obscured by windblown dirt and tumbleweeds.

Shingles hanging beneath porch eaves squawked on rusty chains. The dirt and sand of the desert ticked against the buildings and porch floors and caused a rocking chair to jounce back and forth jerkily, as though an angry ghost were seated in it.

As Hawk rode, the piano's feckless patter grew gradually louder though the moaning wind often obscured it.

A door opened on Hawk's left. A lean, gray-bearded man bound to a wheelchair heaved himself over the doorjamb of the Spotted Horse town marshal's office. A five-pointed star was pinned to his wool shirt, half hidden by his left suspender. He was not only lean but scrawny, his legs appearing withered in his faded denims. He wore a weathered, funnel-brimmed Stetson down low over his eyes. As he came out onto the jailhouse's narrow stoop, his blue-eyed gaze found the tall rider straddling the grulla in the street before him.

The old man stopped instantly. He glanced up the street, toward where a lone horse stood at a hitch rack fronting a saloon, and then glanced once more at the tall stranger in the black frock coat, string tie, and low-crowned, flat-brimmed black hat wielding a Henry rifle and wearing two pistols on his hips.

The town marshal jerked his chair back into the jailhouse and slammed the door.

Hawk looked at the horse standing at the hitch rack a block beyond him, the wind blowing the calico's black tail up under its belly. That's where the piano's din seemed to be originating. He touched spurs to the grulla's flanks and, looking around cautiously, wary of an ambush, continued up the street.

A couple of minutes later, he put his horse up to the right of the calico tied to the hitch rack of the Laughing Lady Saloon, and dismounted. While the two horses touched noses, getting to know each other, Hawk tied the grulla's reins to the hitch rack and then shucked his Henry from its scabbard.

He cast his glance once more toward the opposite side of the street, making sure no bushwhackers were drawing beads on him. He noted nothing more portentous than several windows in which "Closed" signs dangled in the mid-afternoon of a business day.

Hawk looked at the saloon before him, a shabby adobe-brick affair with a brush-roofed gallery. It was indeed from inside this place that someone was trying to play the piano. They'd switched songs now. This one Hawk couldn't recognize. He doubted if anyone could, except possibly the girl who was humming along with it.

Hawk climbed the three steps to the gallery, his spurs trilling. He pushed through the batwings, and stepped to the right quickly so as not to backlight himself.

Loudly, he racked a shell into the Henry's breech as he looked around, his eyes accustomed to quick adjustments from light to dark.

The piano stopped caterwauling. The girl sitting in front of it, on the far side of the bar running along the wall's right side, turned to him. She was clad in a black corset and bustier, with sheer black stockings attached to frilly red garter belts.

She was a pretty, round-faced Mexican with flashing eyes and black feather earrings partly concealed by her long, straight black hair. Her hair was dark enough to make her at least half Indian. Part Apache or Pima, judging by the symmetry of her face, the boldness of her eyes. She had a long, knotted, pink scar running down from the middle of her cheek and ending just beneath her jawline. Its contrast accentuated her beauty.

When the piano's last raucous notes had finished reverberating, Hawk could hear only the wind's keening and muffled voices coming from the ceiling.

The girl was the only one in the long, dingy saloon outfitted with a dozen or so tables and rickety chairs. She rose from the piano bench and, keeping her oblique, dark gaze on Hawk, strolled behind the bar, her high-heeled black shoes tapping on the floor puncheons. The feather earrings danced along her neck.

She stopped about halfway down the bar. She leaned forward on her elbows, giving Hawk a good look at her cleavage, and absently traced the scar with her finger. "Drink?"

Hawk glanced around once more, at the wooden staircase rising at the rear of the room, just beyond the piano. There was a colorfully woven rug at the foot of it, an unlit bracket lamp hanging on the wall over the rug. Above the lamp was the snarling head of a mountain lion.

Hawk glanced at the low ceiling through which the voices continued to filter — one high and shrill, the other low and even.

"That him up there?"

"Him," the girl said, frowning curiously and thoughtfully tapping her right index finger against her lower lip. "Hmmmm. By 'him' do you mean the owner of the calico?"

She may have looked half Indian, but she did not speak in the flat tones of most Natives annunciating English. This girl's English was easy and lilting though touched with a very slight Spanish accent. Raised on the border among several races, most likely.

Hawk stared at her without expression on

his severe-featured, mustached face that betrayed his own mixed bloodline. His father had been a Ute, his mother a Scandinavian immigrant. It was the jade of her eyes that made his own such a contrast to his otherwise aboriginal appearance with beak-like nose and jutting, dimpled chin. Unlike most Indians, however, Hawk's sideburns were thick, and his brushy mustache drooped toward his mouth corners. He kept his dark-brown hair closely cropped.

The girl's mocking half smile faded, and she blinked once slowly as she said, "Doc's with him. Diggin' that bullet out of him. Yours, I take it?"

A shrill cry came hurling down the stairs: "*Ow!* Oh, Christ — that hurt like hell, you old devil!"

The low voice said something Hawk couldn't make out.

The shrill voice said, "Bullshit, you take it easy with that thing or I'll . . ."

The shrill voice trailed off as the other, lower voice said something in calming, reassuring tones.

The girl said, "You'd swear he never took a bullet before."

Hawk moved into the room, loosened the string tie around his neck, and set his rifle

15

down on the table nearest the batwings. "Doesn't sound like I'll be goin' anywhere till that bullet's out of him. I'll take that drink if the offer's still good."

"Offer's good if your money's good."

Hawk kicked out a chair, dug a coin out of his pants pocket, and flipped it off his thumb. It flashed in the window light as it arced toward the girl, who snatched it out of the air with one practiced hand.

She looked at the coin and arched a brow. "For that, you can have a drink, and" — her cheeks dimpled as she offered a lusty smile — "pretty much anything else that ain't nailed down."

"Just the drink will do me for now."

"Whiskey?"

Hawk nodded and doffed his hat as he sagged into his chair. He set the hat down on the table, over his rifle, and raked a hand through his close-shorn hair. He continued to hear the voices in the second story, with an occasional curse and boot stomp, but the hysterics were apparently over.

The girl filled two shot glasses and set them on a wooden tray. She folded a newspaper and set that on the tray, as well, glancing at Hawk and smiling. "Like something to read?"

Hawk shook his head. "Just the drink. Be

pullin' out soon."

"Well, just in case," she said, and moved out from around the bar. As she approached his table, he saw that the corset and bustier were damned near sheer enough to reveal every inch of her nice, full-busted body.

She kept her eyes on him as she set the whiskey in front of him. She set the change from his half eagle down beside the shot glass. She kept the other shot glass on the tray with the folded newspaper as she sat down in a chair across from him.

"Business got slow after he arrived," she said. "It was like the wind blew him in. All the *hombres* who took shelter in here *from* the wind blew on out like the trash being scattered around town." She shook her head once and sipped her whiskey. "Who is he?"

"Clyde Leroy Miller," Hawk said. "Otherwise known as Pima."

"Pretty bad fella, this Pima Miller?"

"About as bad as they come."

She chuckled incredulously. "How bad? Just for conversation's sake and all, since you don't seem to care to take me upstairs and let me earn the rest of that half eagle, which I'm rather good at, if I may say so myself."

Hawk threw back half of his own whiskey, set the glass back down on the table, turned it between his thumb and index finger. Pima Miller and the sawbones were still talking, so he didn't mind sitting here chinning with the whore. He had a mind to take her upstairs.

His loins were heavy, for he hadn't been with a woman in weeks. But he couldn't chance losing his edge.

Not this afternoon, with his quarry near.

Hawk said, "He and his gang robbed the bank in Kingman. Shot the president, vice president, locked the customers inside, and burned the place to the ground. They shot the Kingman marshal on their way out of town, dropped two posse members the next day."

"You're the posse now?"

"Close enough."

"Lawman?"

"That's right."

"Where's your badge?"

Hawk slid the lapel of his black frock coat to one side, revealing his sun-and-moon deputy US marshal's badge. The whore leaned forward slightly in her chair, frowned as she studied the three ounces of tin-plated copper.

"I hate to tell you this," she said with a dubious look. "But you're wearin' it upside down."

"Yep."

Her look was skeptical. "May I ask why?"

"It's an upside-down world . . . full of upside-down laws."

"And you're an upside-down lawman . . . ?"

"Houndin' upside-down owlhoots." Hawk grinned as he threw back the last of his shot.

She studied him, nodding slowly, tentatively. Of course, she'd spied the glint of madness in his keen, jade eyes. Most did eventually. Some sooner than others.

Hawk was well aware it was there, for he'd seen it while shaving in a looking glass and hadn't been one bit surprised or bothered. It had come with the black territory he'd begun riding in the forever-dark days in the wake of his son's murder and his wife's self-hanging. Linda had hanged herself from the tree in their backyard right after Jubal's funeral.

The whore glanced at the stairs to her right. "Where's the rest of his bunch?"

"Feedin' mountain lions and coyotes along the trail between here and Kingman, Miss . . ."

"Vivienne."

"Wildcats gotta eat, too, Miss Vivienne."

"And you're . . . ?"

Hawk dipped his chin, narrowed his jade

eyes. "The upside-down lawman who's about to drill a bullet through your pretty head, Miss Vivienne."

CHAPTER 2
SAWBONES WANTED

Hawk stared at the whore sitting across the table from him.

Vivienne stared back at him, her eyes intense. Hawk glanced down at the tray sitting just right of her half-empty shot glass. She had her hand beneath the folded newspaper atop the tray.

"Shoot me?" she said, wrinkling the skin above the bridge of her nose. "Why on earth would you do such a nasty thing, Mister Upside-down Lawman?"

"Slide your hand very slowly out from beneath that newspaper."

"What?"

Hawk waited. Her eyes flickered slightly. Color rose in her pretty cheeks, the scar turning paler, as she slid her hand slowly out from under the newspaper. She slid the hand over the lip of the tray and over the edge of the table to her lap.

Hawk reached across the table and flipped

21

the newspaper off of the tray. A small, black, double-barreled pocket pistol with ivory grips glared up at him — a very small but very deadly coiled snake.

The girl grabbed her right forearm with her other hand and sort of scrunched her shoulders together, pooching her lips out and averting her gaze from Hawk's.

Hawk picked up the gun. He flicked the loading gate open and spun the cylinder, letting all five cartridges plunk to the table, where they rolled. Then he tossed the gun over the batwings, which the wind was jostling, and into the street.

"How much did he pay you?"

Vivienne shrugged, smiled bashfully, and again traced the scar with her finger. "A half eagle."

Hawk gave an ironic chuff. Then he turned toward the stairs, and frowned.

No more sounds were coming from the second story.

Apprehension was a cold finger pressed to the small of the rogue lawman's back. He stared at the ceiling, ears pricked. No sound except the wind's moaning and the ratcheting clicks of the batwings.

"What room's he in?" Hawk asked Vivienne.

"Three."

Hawk picked up the Henry, glanced at the girl staring up at him gravely. "One peep out of you . . . ," he said softly, menacingly.

Vivienne turned her mouth corners down.

Hawk strode quickly to the stairs. He climbed the steps two at a time, stopped at the landing and, holding the rifle up high across his chest, looked up toward the second floor.

Nothing.

He climbed the second landing and stopped at the top. To his right and on the left side of the dim hall carpeted with a soiled red runner, a door stood partway open. He moved slowly, one step at a time, wincing at each creak of the floor beneath the runner, to the half-open door.

He kicked the door wide and stood crouched over the Henry, which he extended straight out from his right hip, sliding it quickly from right to left and back again. The room smelled like sweat, blood, and whiskey. The lone, brass-framed bed, which nearly filled the small room, was rumpled, sheets bloodstained.

A gray-headed man in a black suit sat in a chair near the bed's right-front corner, beside an open window. The man's head was tipped to his chest, as though he were sleeping though he wore spectacles and a

23

stethoscope.

He looked as though someone had splashed him with a full bucket of red paint.

Hawk moved to him in two quick, long strides and pushed his head up and back with his rifle barrel, revealing the wide, deep gash stretching from one ear to the other. The cut was so deep that Hawk could see the man's spine through pale sinews and liver-colored muck. A bloody scalpel lay on the floor near his blood-splattered shoes.

Hawk let the dead pill roller's head drop back down to his chest and crouched to look out the window beside him.

A hay wagon was just then making its way along the main street, two beefy mules in the traces. A gray-bearded old man in overalls was shaking the reins over the mules' backs.

Wind tore at the hay in the wagon box. There was a deep depression in the hay pile. As the wagon passed from Hawk's right to his left, Hawk saw a murky, black-hatted figure in a light-blue shirt, suspenders, and black neckerchief running down a cross street, bits of hay clinging to his boots.

Hawk grimaced as he raised the Henry to his shoulder, aimed quickly, and fired. The rifle leaped and roared, setting Hawk's ears to ringing in the close confines of the hotel room. The bullet blew up dust about six inches behind the heel of Pima Miller's scissoring right boot.

The killer glanced over his shoulder as Hawk ejected the spent cartridge casing. Hawk aimed again, squeezed the Henry's trigger, and watched his second bullet plume dust about a foot in front of where the last one had, another four inches shy of its mark.

And then Hawk could have sworn that Pima Miller cast him a taunting grin over his left shoulder as the outlaw continued running in a shambling, wounded sort of way, and disappeared around the rear corner of an old adobe church.

Hawk raked out a curse as he swung around and ran out of the room. He dropped down the stairs threes steps at a time, raising a ruckus that sounded like thunderclaps. Vivienne stood by the piano she'd been playing earlier, wringing her hands together in front of her see-through corset and regarding Hawk warily.

"I do apologize," Hawk grunted as he ran past the girl on his way toward the front of the Laughing Lady.

"What for?" the girl called after him.

"The town's out a sawbones!"

Hawk tipped his head low against the

howling wind and ran up the street to the west. He ran one block and then turned into the cross street and sprinted for the back of the church.

He took his time scouring the area behind the church for Pima Miller, wary of an ambush. But then he crossed a rocky arroyo and found a little adobe shack and a stable and stock pen sitting in a clearing among wind-jostled mesquites and palo verdes. A corral of cottonwood poles flanked the shack, with a half dozen or so horses milling under a brush arbor.

Goats bleated in the stock pen. Dust rose and swirled, peppered with hay as well as the shit from goats, chickens, and horses.

Hawk stopped at the edge of the wash, facing the farmyard. The shack was no larger than the goat pen. It was cracked and discolored and several of the ironwood branches forming its roof lifted in the wind.

As Hawk surveyed the shack, a man stepped out of its front door, ducking his head and then donning his hat. He carried a rifle in his right hand. His long, cream-colored duster blew in the wind.

Another man stepped out behind him, also ducking through the low door and donning his hat. Two more men followed the second one, and a minute later, Hawk was

26

facing five men armed with rifles. Four stood over six feet tall. The second man from the left was a full head shorter and dressed all in black leather except for a billowy red neckerchief whipping around in the gale.

Black mustaches drooped down over his mouth corners. He was the only one of the five not holding a rifle but held his hands over the two .45s on his hips.

None of these men was Pima Miller. Hawk guessed that Miller was holed up inside the shack from which the raucous strains of a baby's cries were whipped and torn by the wind.

Hawk recognized a couple of the hard-eyed, bearded faces from the wanted dodgers residing in his saddlebags. Two of these men he knew for sure had prices on their heads. They probably all did. But that didn't matter to Hawk. He'd take the bounty money; he'd be foolish not to. He and his horse had to eat, same as everyone else.

But mostly these men needed killing and Gideon Hawk believed he'd been placed on this earth to do just that — kill men who needed killing. It was as if some judicious spook whispered in his ear which ones needed killing and which ones did not.

Rare it was that Hawk's trail led to a man who did not need a bullet in his head, however. Some needed two, just to be sure. And none needed proper burials. If such men had been placed here for a reason at all, it could be only to feed the carrion eaters.

The man standing to the right of the short, black-clad *hombre* stared incredulously at the rogue lawman, and said, "Gideon *Hawk* . . . ?"

Hawk said, "You had to know our paths would cross sooner or later, Frye."

Leonard Frye — wanted for sundry offenses including bank robbery and murder. He'd also raped a young schoolteacher near the creek by which she'd taken her class for a picnic.

"Why's that?" Frye asked.

" 'Cause when a man needs killing as badly as you do, and for as long as you have, it's what I'd call *inevitable.*"

The short man glanced at Leonard Frye and said something out of the corner of his mouth. Hawk couldn't hear the words but he did hear Frye's response: "Shut up."

The last man to the right of the group scrunched up his face and said, "What — you think you're God or somethin'?"

"Yeah," Hawk said. "Somethin' like that."

Inside the shack, the baby continued to cry. Hawk kept one eye on the open door and the shuttered windows, wary of Pima Miller flinging a shot at him.

Leonard Frye opened and closed his hands around the Winchester he held across his chest. He shaped a cockeyed grin, narrowing one eye. "Five against one, Hawk!"

As Hawk snapped his rifle to his shoulder, he said, "Nope — just four, Leonard!"

He drilled a round, black hole in the middle of Leonard Frye's forehead. Frye didn't make a sound as Hawk's bullet snapped his head back sharply and sent him staggering, hang-jawed, dead on his feet, dropping his rifle. The others jerked to immediate life, but Hawk dropped the short man before the little man could snap off a single round with his fancy .45s.

And then, as the others opened up on him, Hawk pivoted to his right and dove behind a dilapidated handcart moldering at the base of a barrel cactus. Slugs splatted into the side of the handcart and plowed up dirt and sand around Hawk. One bullet tore through the rotten handcart to sear a short line across his right cheek.

Hawk rolled away from the handcart to the other side of the barrel cactus. The three remaining shooters stood crouched and firing their rifles from their hips.

They'd lost track of Hawk for three vital seconds. The rogue lawman took advantage by shooting out from the right side of the barrel cactus. His aim was muddy from this position, however, and he managed to clip one man only in the knee. By the time he'd emptied the Henry, he'd wounded only one more. Tossing the empty rifle aside, he pulled both pistols.

Lead hammered the ground in front of him.

The smell of cordite was pepper on the breeze.

Hawk pulled his head back behind the cactus as two bullets plunked into it, spraying pulp and thorns. Hawk triggered his Russian around the cactus's left side. The bullet clanked off a rifle and plowed into the jaw of one of the shooters, who screamed and dropped his weapon as he buried his face in his hands.

The two others were backing up, eyes bright with anxiety, apparently looking for cover behind them.

Hawk aimed his Colt carefully around the right side of the cactus, and drilled one of the retreaters in the belly. As that man folded like a jackknife, bellowing curses, Hawk drilled the other one in the left shoulder. As the man screamed and jerked back, Hawk's Colt leaped and roared again. The bullet slammed into the man's neck, just right of his Adam's apple.

The shooter dropped his rifle and twisted around and fell. He rolled over onto his back, rose to a half-sitting position, and tried bringing his rifle up once more.

Hawk gained a knee, aimed the Colt carefully. The wounded shooter stared at him, terror in his wide-open eyes. He opened his mouth to scream. The rogue lawman's next shot shattered the man's front teeth and shredded his tongue before blowing out the back of his head.

Spying movement near the cabin, Hawk jerked his head toward the door to see Pima Miller grinning at him over the Remington he was aiming straight out in his right hand. Miller's gloved left hand was clamped over the bloodstain just above his left hip.

Hawk pulled his head back behind the cactus, and Miller's slug went hurling through the air where Hawk's face had been a quarter second before.

Hawk fired both his pistols toward the cabin.

Miller gritted his teeth as he jerked back inside, and then he was gone, nothing but dark doorway where he'd been.

And then Hawk was running toward the open door with both pistols cocked and raised.

Inside, the baby was screaming louder.

CHAPTER 3
MOTHER AND CHILD

Hawk bolted through the open door, threw himself to the right, and pressed his back against the wall. He knocked a shelf loose of its moorings, and the shelf and several clay containers and airtight tins crashed to the floor.

Ignoring the din, the rogue lawman shifted both his aimed pistols around, looking for a target in the shack's rough-hewn, sparsely furnished, dingy interior. The shack was long and deep.

At the rear were two windows. The right window's shutter was open. In the yard beyond it, Miller was gaining his feet, looking back through the window at Hawk. He was smiling but his unshaven cheeks appeared drawn and haggard. His long, cinnamon mustaches beneath the beak-like nose and close-set eyes were buffeting in the wind.

The wounded killer raised his Remington,

and Hawk ducked as the pistol stabbed flames toward him, popping flatly. The slug slammed into the wall over Hawk's crouching body.

Hawk rose, raising his pistols to his shoulder. He held fire. Pima Miller was no longer in the window.

Hawk bolted forward. He ran between a cluttered wooden eating table and the wall on the right, past what he thought was a person slumped on a sofa and a crate hanging from the ceiling by ropes. This crate was where the baby's cries seemed to be originating.

None of these messages that Hawk's senses were sending to his brain seemed very significant at the moment. His gaze was riveted on the window beyond which he'd seen Pima Miller.

As Hawk reached the window, he stopped and aimed his Russian out the opening. A small adobe barn and corral lay about sixty yards away, amid low shrubs, cacti, and blowing grit. The horses were standing beneath the brush arbor, their tails blowing in the wind.

Another horse — this one saddled — was tied to the corral gate. A burlap feed sack hung from its ears. Another horse was galloping off through shrubs flanking the corral's right side. As the horse and rider — Pima Miller in his blue shirt and black hat — swung to the right, following a shallow wash, Hawk aimed quickly at the obscured figure, and fired.

Miller and the horse were twisting and turning too violently down the wash for accurate shooting. Hawk's slugs plumed dust, spanged off rocks, and snapped mesquite branches.

Hearing himself curse loudly, Hawk continued firing, with both pistols now leaping in his hands, until the hammers clicked benignly against the firing pins.

He loosed another bellowing curse as he stared off toward where Pima Miller had been only a few seconds before and where there was only blowing grit and jostling branches. The horse tied to the corral gate shook its feed sack free of its ears, shook its head again, and whinnied.

Behind Hawk, the baby was crying loudly, shrilly.

He remembered the slumped figure.

He walked back along the table cluttered with all manner of weapon — pistols, rifles, and knives — as well as ammunition of several calibers. There were plates with food on them, a board with a half a loaf of crumbly brown bread, a pot of beans, a saucer bearing goat cheese.

But Hawk's attention wasn't on the cluttered table but on the figure slumped across the red velvet fainting couch which, with its scrolled arms and legs, looked as out of place here as would a zebra in the corral out back.

The girl was hanging half off of the couch's left side, her head on the floor, arms dangling. She wore a cheap, green dress of embroidered cotton. Her feet were bare, brown legs dirty. Hawk dropped to a knee beside the girl hanging off the arm of the couch, and cleared his throat tentatively.

"Miss . . . ?"

When he received no response, he took her arms and pulled her to a sitting position atop the couch. He immediately saw why she hadn't responded. There was a ragged-edged hole in her forehead, sort of centered between the bridge of her nose and her left eye.

Her large, brown eyes were open and staring at Hawk's chest. Long, straight, raven hair hung down past her shoulders and along her slender, brown arms. An Apache girl, judging by her skin color and the broad flatness and rounded cheekbones of her pretty face.

She wore a doubled necklace of .45-

caliber cartridges strung with braided horsehair around her neck. The cartridges winked dully in the dull light from the window at the end of the room — the window through which Hawk had let Pima Miller flee.

The baby continued to cry loudly, stridently. So loudly at times that Hawk's eardrums rattled and ached. Feeling as though someone had stuck a stiletto in his guts, the rogue lawman stepped over to the crate hanging by ropes from two rusty hooks in the ceiling.

The peach crate was padded with a folded, striped blanket — part of a horse blanket. The little brown child inside the crate lay crying up at Hawk, its tiny, round, brown face crumpled in misery. The child — a boy, Hawk thought — squeezed his eyes shut with every bellowing scream. There was a momentary pause in the screams as the child filled its tiny lungs, and then the screams resumed.

The boy's tiny hands, each little larger than the tip of Hawk's own fingers, flailed in the air between the boy and Hawk.

Flailed for the comfort of its mother . . .

"Nan-tee."

The voice sounding just off of Hawk's right shoulder caused him to jerk with a start. He turned to see Vivienne standing beside him, staring at the dead woman sitting on the fainting couch. The saloon girl held a blanket around her bare shoulders.

"Nan-tee," Vivienne said. "Miller's woman."

"That his, too?" Hawk nodded toward the child in the peach crate.

Vivienne nodded. She reached into the peach crate, wrapped her hands around the child clad in an oilskin diaper, and lifted him out of the box. She pressed the boy's tear-streaked cheek to her own scarred cheek and then held him fast against her breast, rocking him gently.

Hawk tore his beleaguered gaze from the child to the boy's dead mother.

"Miller?" Vivienne said.

"Out the window," Hawk said tonelessly.

The child had stopped crying. The silence now on the lee side of the gunfire and the infant's wails was funereal. Outside, the wind howled and moaned like a hungry, stalking animal.

"He left her here," Hawk said. "Left the boy here."

"That is understandable," Vivienne said, continuing to rock the child gently. "He is a bastard. A *pendejo*. I never knew what she saw in him — Nan-tee. She was always fond of the outlaws, though. The rest of the town was scared of her . . . because of *them.*" She looked around at the small shack cluttered with food, guns, tack, and ammunition. "Scared of this place."

"This where they holed up — Miller's bunch?"

"For two, three weeks at a time," Vivienne said, and then cooed to the child who had taken comfort in the saloon girl's touch.

"They would ride in, and business would dry up in Spotted Horse, just as it has done for the past week, since they last rode in." Vivienne stared at him for a time, frown lines cut across her light-brown forehead, above her curious brown eyes.

"Who are you?" she whispered.

"The man who killed the child's mother," Hawk said again in the same hollow, toneless voice as before, as he continued to stare at the child nuzzling Vivienne's breast, trying to get to the nipple behind the see-through corset. Some invisible specter was turning that stiletto in his guts, probing around inside him as though fishing for his heart.

Wretched damned world . . .

"I know a woman who will care for him," Vivienne said as thunder rumbled in the distance, beneath the wind. "He will be better off without her and Miller."

"No child is better off without his ma," Hawk said.

Vivienne turned and walked out of the shack, gently rocking the child against her chest.

Hawk stared down at Nan-tee. As the dead woman, her hair blowing in the wind funneling through the shack, stared blindly across the room, he had a vision of his own wife's face as Linda had dangled from that big cottonwood in their backyard in the little, Midwestern town of Crossroads, in the miserable hours after they'd buried their son who too had been hanged.

Only Jubal had been hanged by Three-Fingers Ned Meade as payback against Hawk. Before he'd gone rogue because of Meade and the crooked county prosecutor who had turned Meade free on a technicality he'd found in the law, Hawk had brought Meade's perverted younger brother to justice.

Linda had hanged herself out of grief.

Nan-tee's face was now Linda's face, framed in tousled, yellow-blonde hair, staring at him as though pleading with him to forgive her for not being strong enough to live in this world without their boy.

Hawk drew a deep, raspy breath. He

raised his hands to his face, raked them down his cheeks, rubbing away the tears.

Then he turned away from the dead woman, and followed Vivienne and the child back across the wash.

As Hawk approached the Laughing Lady, he stopped in the middle of the street, which was empty except for blowing dust and tumbleweeds. Vivienne walked out of the saloon, the child in her arms wrapped in a green army blanket. The whore had changed into baggy denims and a wool shirt, a green bandanna wrapped over her head.

She moved down the porch steps and untied Pima Miller's horse from the hitch rack. She sidled the horse to the porch steps, climbed to the top step, and stepped into the saddle.

She swung the calico toward Hawk, cradling the child in one arm against her chest. She canted her head toward the Laughing Lady. "Help yourself. I won't be long."

She pointed the horse west and rammed the heels of her moccasin-clad feet against the horse's ribs. The calico lunged forward and galloped out of the windblown town, the girl's long, black hair blowing out behind her.

Hawk looked at his grulla for a full minute before he actually saw the horse. Practical matters returned to him, washing up behind the patina of the dead Nan-tee in his head, and he led the horse off to the Spotted Horse Livery & Feed Barn, which he'd noticed when he'd first ridden into town.

He paid the young Mexican who ran the place to stable and care for his horse. He paid him an extra eagle to drag away the outlaws lying in the yard outside of Nan-tee's adobe. He instructed the liveryman to leave them in a draw far enough downwind of town that their scent wouldn't foul the air in Spotted Horse.

He paid him an extra eagle to bury Nan-tee in the yard behind her cabin.

Whatever the Apache woman had been, she'd been the baby's mother, as well, and to Hawk's mind that set her nominally above the carrion feeders.

Then he went back to the Laughing Lady and drained half a bottle of whiskey, sitting out on the porch, watching large, sooty storm clouds roll in from the west. Near nightfall, when the rain had started, the wind howling in earnest and the thunder clapping brutally, causing the saloon's timbers to creek, Vivienne rode back into town.

The baby was no longer with her.

She stabled the horse, returned to the saloon, and carried a fresh bottle and two glasses out onto the porch. She sat down beside Hawk, wrapped in her blanket, both legs curled beneath her, and they drank together and stared out into the rain-lashed, stormy night.

Neither said a word even after they'd gone upstairs together.

CHAPTER 4
RIDER ON THE STORM

Sitting atop a low hill beneath a wind-lashed palo verde, the coyote watched the figure slowly take shape out of the early darkness and hammering rain.

At first, the coyote thought the rider might be a sick deer or a gimpy burro that had strayed away from some miner's diggings. He might be able to take down such a beast and chew out the liver and bladder to carry back to his burrow and dine in relative comfort, out of the thundering storm.

The coyote, wet and bedraggled, its tail curled forward around its left back leg, pricked its ears and worked its nose, all senses alert as it stared at the moving figure.

As the silhouette beyond the slanting, white javelins of the rain mounted a low hill about fifty yards from the coyote's hill, the coyote saw that what he had been watching and hoping would be a meal was, to its dismay, a horse and a human rider. The coyote smelled the horse now, though the beast of human burden was downwind from the coyote, and it smelled the copper smell of blood.

The man's blood.

The coyote had smelled such blood before, as well as the blood of young wild horses that he and his pack had taken down when the coyote itself was young. The man was injured, but he was mounted safely atop the horse that continued plodding toward the coyote.

As the horse and low-hunkered rider continued plodding toward the coyote, the coyote gave a disgruntled mewl deep in its throat, turned, ducked under a low-hanging branch of the palo verde, and loped off down the backside of the hill.

It faded into the storm, hoping to maybe find a drowned fawn in one of the flooded arroyos.

Pima Miller, dozing in the saddle, had felt the horse stop. Now he looked over the dun's head to see what had halted it.

An arroyo stretched across the desert path about twenty yards ahead. Through the thin line of storm-beaten willows and mesquites, Miller saw the butterscotch water sliding between the banks that appeared to have a twenty-, maybe thirty-yard gap between them.

Occasional leafy branches went bobbing past, twisting and turning with the current.

In the stormy sky, lightning flashed. Thunder peeled like a malevolent god slapping his hands together and laughing.

Miller looked down at his left side. Just above his hip, blood mixed with the rain. It was oozing out of the hole in his shirt. The wound, two days old, felt like a rat was trying to chew its way out of him.

He'd had no idea who'd been dogging him until Frye had identified him back at Nan-tee's place.

Gideon Hawk, otherwise known as the rogue lawman.

Persistent damned son of a bitch!

Miller lifted his head, and water sluiced off the brim to tumble down his back and onto his saddle, soaking him further though he probably couldn't get much wetter than he already was. He'd left Spotted Horse two hours ago, and the rain had started soon after. A summer monsoon. It could rain all night.

Miller needed shelter.

The sawbones in Spotted Horse had dug the bullet out of his hide, but he hadn't sewn the wound closed. Miller hadn't time for that. The son of a bitch who'd been dog-ging him for the past four days, killing Wayne and Pierson and T. J. and then Dick Overcast, was warming his heels.

Now the outlaw needed a ranch cabin or a goat herder's shack. Even a cave would do. Anywhere he could hole up out of the weather and catch a couple hours of shut-eye.

Miller straightened his back, clamping his left hand to the wound in his side, and rammed his spurs into the dun's flanks.

"Come on, you ewe-necked hammer-head!" the outlaw bellowed savagely into the wind. The horse leaped ahead at the man's sudden, angry onslaught. "Let's get across that arroyo!"

The horse trotted through the trees and stopped at the edge of the water, furiously shaking its head.

"He-yahhh!" Miller bellowed.

He hadn't needed to. A sudden thunder burst, sounding like that dark god pounding an empty, giant steel barrel with an ax handle, nudged the frightened beast on into the stream. Almost instantly, the horse was in up to its neck, the cold, dirty water clos-ing up over Miller's legs. As it reached his crotch, he sucked a breath through gritted teeth and shuddered.

47

He felt the horse working furiously beneath him, grunting and whickering, trying to keep moving, to keep its head above the water.

"Come on, goddamnit!" the outlaw shouted, half the sentence drowned by another thunderclap, which came about two seconds off the heels of a lightning flash so close that Miller thought he could smell brimstone above the fresh, muddy scent of the sodden desert.

The horse was sliding downstream faster than it was moving forward. Fury burned through the pain-racked outlaw. He whipped his rein ends against the mount's right hip. That caused the horse to lurch beneath him.

Miller was about to lash the beast again but stopped when three crossed witches' fingers of lightning flashed just ahead and left. The pink, blue-limned strike was so near, it lit up the roiling stream for one full second — long enough for Miller to see that the arroyo was at least twice as wide as he'd first thought it was.

"Holy shit!" he yelled, fear ensconcing him in its large, chill hand.

This wasn't no average wash. A wash out here that wide had to be Jackass Gulch — a killer when it came to gully washers like the one Miller now found himself in the midst of.

"Come on, you cayuse!" the outlaw bellowed, whipping the horse's left hip without mercy, grinding his spurs against the mount's flanks.

The horse lunged forward once, twice, three times. Then Miller heard it give what sounded like a giant yawn. Only he knew it was a groan that meant the horse was done for.

"Shit!" Miller cried as the horse, too weak to swim any longer against such a raging current, began sliding nearly straight down the center of the stream.

The horse sort of fluttered in the water. It dropped a good foot, and then suddenly Miller found himself floating on top of the saddle, his boots slipping free of the stirrups and his legs sliding out from beneath him.

He fought for the saddle horn, but suddenly the horse dropped farther beneath him. It turned onto its side, and Miller flailed with all his limbs, trying desperately to stay above the current. Then, like a helping hand, something solid and black swept toward him. He'd barely glimpsed it, whatever it was, riding low in the water before him, and he gave a soggy grunt as he threw both arms up.

They caught the tree, hooked around the trunk that was about as large around as his own torso. It stopped him abruptly. Wet bark ground into his nose and forehead. A broken point of the tree stabbed his side about six inches beneath his armpit. He smiled at the pain because it only meant that he had something solid to hold onto, something he could ride down the arroyo until he could find his way to one of the banks.

As he clung to the tree, however, he realized he wasn't moving. He glanced to his left. Another lightning flash revealed the muddy bank out from which the tree extended. Apparently, the wind had torn it out of the ground by its roots.

He'd been thrown a buoy!

Grinding his teeth against the pain in his left side, Miller walked his hands along the side of the fallen cottonwood, slowly making his way, handhold by handhold, to the bank. As he did, the rain continued to pour down on him. The skies rumbled and clapped demonically. Lightning flashed so brightly that at times he was blinded. The darkness between flashes was surreal.

His boots scraped against the bank beneath the water. Continuing to crawl along the side of the tree, Miller made his way up the bank. When his legs were nearly out of the water, he climbed the rest of the four feet through the mud and sodden gravel to the top and lay there for a time, cheek to the earth, catching his breath and sending a silent prayer to whatever dark god had saved his worthless hide.

He chuckled.

The chuckle died on his lips, however, when he remembered the cold-eyed bastard who'd been dogging him. He looked behind and out beyond the tree extending into the wash, which was narrower here than it had been upstream, and probed the rainy night for signs that Gideon Hawk had followed him.

Nothing moved but the wind and the rain and the water sliding behind him, occasionally whipped to a creamy froth.

Most men wouldn't follow in weather like this. But Miller had heard Hawk's reputation. Most men on the frontier, especially *outlaw* men, were well aware of the green-eyed half-breed who wore the deputy US marshal's badge upside down on his vest.

The crazy-loco son of a bitch who went around killing outlaws like they were rats scurrying around a trash dump. The man was worse than the lowest of bounty

51

hunters.

Hawk didn't hunt men for the bounty on their heads. He hunted them to kill them for his own demonic satisfaction.

It was said that the loco son of a bitch, in his own messed-up mind, was still killing the man who'd hanged his boy. Over and over again, with each outlaw Hawk murdered, he was killing "Three-Fingers" Ned Meade.

Over and over and over again . . .

Miller shuddered from an extra chill, just thinking about the rogue lawman out there somewhere in the murky darkness, hunting him with the sure-footed, cold-blooded, razor-edged senses of a stalking puma.

Miller filled his lungs and yelled across the wash behind him, "I ain't Three-Fingers Ned, you son of a bitch! He's *dead*! You done *killed* him, for chrissakes!"

Miller sucked a damp breath, chuckled again. He himself was getting crazier than a tree full of owls. Hawk wasn't out here. He was probably still holed up in Spotted Horse, waiting for the storm to break.

"Damn fool," Miller admonished himself, groaning against his sundry miseries as he heaved himself to his feet.

He looked around and then slogged off through the willows and cottonwoods, the storm-tossed trees and shrubs dancing around him like drunken witches. He didn't know how long he'd walked, practically dragging his boot toes, before he came to a trail.

He studied the trail beneath his boots carefully for a time. It was a graded trace scored with deep wheel furrows. Many of them. Of course, the furrows were filled with water now, and the rain was splashing into them like bullets fired from heaven, but they were furrows, just the same.

Miller's heart quickened hopefully. He'd come to the Butterfield stage road. At last, he had a trail to follow. Trails lead somewhere. This trail would lead to a settlement, eventually.

He'd taken only twenty or thirty steps before he stopped again. He'd spied something off the trail's left side.

Lights.

The silhouettes of buildings shifted amid the lights. Then Miller heard what sounded like the clattering of a windmill's blades.

He saw the sign slanting in the mud along the trail, beside a tall saguaro: SUPERSTITION RELAY STATION.

Miller swerved from the trail and entered what he now saw was a broad yard. The windmill lay just ahead and right, clattering raucously beneath the storm's din. Just beyond lay a long, low cabin, its lamp-lit windows beckoning.

Miller grinned. He brushed his hand across the holster thonged on his right thigh. His Remington was still snugged down in the sodden leather. The cartridges were likely so damp they wouldn't fire, but the people in the cabin wouldn't know that.

"Halloo the cabin!" Miller laughed, his words swallowed by the thunder. "Wet and weary traveler out here!"

CHAPTER 5
THE GIRL AT
SUPERSTITION STATION

Miller was glad there was no dog in the station yard.

If there had been, he'd no doubt be aware of it by now, as he quietly mounted the steps of the front stoop that sat on stone pylons. The dog would likely be nipping at his heels and raising one hell of a ruckus, ruining the outlaw's chance at surprising those within.

Miller didn't hate dogs, but dogs were almost never an outlaw's friend.

His Remington in his right hand, Miller moved to the window to the right of the front door. There was a thin red curtain that Miller could see through. Staring through the sashed pane, he grinned. And then he moved back to the door.

He opened the screen door, held it open with his right boot, and then tripped the metal latch of the inside door with his left hand.

When the latch clicked, he cocked the

Remy, drew the door open, and stepped inside quickly, pulling the door closed behind him.

The girl sitting at the long, wooden table to Miller's left jerked her head toward him, and gasped. She'd been wrapping wet rawhide around a pick handle, but now she raised both hands from the table as she started to rise from the bench.

A long-haired old man had his back to Miller. He must have been hard of hearing. He apparently hadn't heard the door open or the trill of Miller's spurs as the outlaw had stepped over the doorjamb. Only when the girl, crouched over the table and staring wide-eyed at the intruder, said, "Uh . . . um . . . old man — I think we got *company!*" did the oldster turn his head to look over his left shoulder.

He dropped the coffee mug he'd just refilled from a black pot. As the mug hit the braided rug beneath the old man's boots with a dull thunk, the oldster reached for a double-barreled shotgun leaning against a ceiling post.

"No, no, no," Pima Miller said, wagging his head and trying not to shiver against the cold that had penetrated his bones. "Now, why would you want to go and shoot a weary traveler on such a cold, wet night?"

The old man forestalled his movement toward the shotgun, and turned full around to face Miller. He had a big, craggy, warty face, with a blue-gray Vandyke beard that accented the ruddiness of his sun-seared cheeks. His pale-blue eyes flashed angrily as he said, "Maybe on account o' that weary traveler comin' in here unannounced and holdin' a pistol on me!"

His voice was hoarse, raspy with age and tobacco smoke. He had a coal-black wart, large as a coat button, beneath his right eye.

A hissing sounded.

At first, Miller thought the girl had made it. But then he saw on the other end of the table, beyond a pile of miscellaneous leather and burlap pack gear, a large cat. It was standing on the table, its back humped, and it was glaring at Miller and hissing raucously.

It was no ordinary cat. This one was twice the size of your average larger-than-average kitty, and its ears were tufted. It head was large and round, eyes glowing like copper pennies.

"Christ!" Miller said, swinging the Remy toward the beast. "You got a damn *bobcat* in here?"

The girl said, "Don't shoot, ya damn fool. He's friendly!"

"Don't look friendly to me!"

The girl looked at the cat. "Claws, pipe down!"

"Yeah. Pipe down, Claws!" Miller said through gritted teeth — or he would have gritted them if they hadn't been clattering so violently — "or I'll drill a forty-four round through your mangy hide!"

"Claws!" the girl yelled, hooking her thumb over her left shoulder.

The cat leaped down from the table with a solid thump and dashed up a narrow wooden staircase beyond a fieldstone fire-place in which flames danced. The stairs led to a loft. The cat dashed into the loft and plopped down to stare through the cottonwood-pole rail above the kitchen.

The cat's copper eyes glowed menacingly beneath the silhouettes of its tufted ears.

"Who in the hell has a bobcat for a pet?" Miller said in disgust, waving his cocked pistol around, wondering what other surprises lay in store for him here. "Anymore o' them things?"

"No, he's the only one," the girl said.

"Any dogs?"

"No, the old man don't like dogs."

"Any other *people* here?"

"Nope," the old man said, holding his disdainful gaze on the interloper from the

58

other side of the table.

"Any hostlers out in the barn?"

"I'm the only hostler here," the old man said. "The line's too cheap to hire more."

"When's the next stage due?"

"Not till tomorrow," the girl said. "Likely won't get through till the next day, with this weather an' all." She gave a saucy, mocking smile as her hazel eyes raked Miller's soggy frame up and down. "But I guess you know all about that, don't you?"

"Jodi, quit talkin' to this man!" the old man ordered.

"You're the one best shut up!" Miller stomped around the table. His icy glare caused the old man — he had to be pushing seventy — to move his Adam's apple up and down in his stringy neck and take one step back toward the range.

Miller set his pistol on the end of the table and picked up the double-barreled shotgun — a cheap, Belgium-made affair stamped Cambridge Arms Co. A twelve-gauge, it was a side-by-side hammer gun. Miller breeched it. Both barrels were filled with live shells.

He snapped it closed, shoved his Remington back down in its holster, and aimed the shotgun at the old man's pendulous belly. "Now, how 'bout I blow a hole through you, old man?"

"Ah, shit!" the old man complained, raising his hands to his shoulders. "You got no cause to do that. Take what you want and go!"

Miller looked at the girl, who was still standing in front of the table. She stood only an inch or so over five feet, but she was about as comely as they came. Not much over seventeen, if that, and her pretty, heart-shaped, hazel-eyed face was framed by thick, tawny curls. She was dressed in a coarse work shirt and overalls, but the body beneath those crude duds was well filled out in all the best places.

She blushed under the outlaw's scrutiny.

"Except her!" the old man snarled. "You can't have her!"

"She yours?"

"Yes, she's mine. She's my *granddaughter*. She belongs to me, and if you touch one hair on her head . . ." The old man seemed to realize the ridiculousness of his threat. He swallowed again and looked at the twelve-gauge in Miller's hands.

Miller laughed. Then he shuddered as the cold continued to rack him, and turned to the old man. "Whiskey!"

"I ain't got no whiskey!" The old man lowered his voice, and his right eye flashed shrewdly. "I got bacanora. That'll take the chill out of your bones . . . if you're man enough."

"Oh, don't give me that shit, you old fool. Break out the bacanora, for chrissakes." Miller looked at the girl. "Was he born a fool or did he get this way in his old age?"

"He's been a fool for as long as I've known him." The girl glanced at the old man jeeringly.

The old man glanced back at her, swelling his nostrils, as he reached toward a high shelf above the dry sink right of the range. "I told you not to talk to him. You mind me!"

"You shut up, old man. Just pour me a tall one and sit down at that table and keep your hands up where I can keep an eye on 'em. You try anything, I'll blast you, and this girl won't be your concern no more."

Miller cut his eyes to her again. Again, her cheeks flushed, though she otherwise betrayed no expression.

"Oh, I know you will," the old man said, pouring out the grapefruit-colored agave-derived alcohol into a tin cup and sliding it across the table to Miller. "I know who you are. I recognized you as soon as you came in here."

"You did? Who am I?"

"Pima Miller."

Miller sipped the bacanora. It punched the back of his throat like a fist wrapped in barbed-wire then pulverized his vocal chords as it raked down into his belly to burn holes through his stomach lining. He choked out, "No, shit — I *am*?"

"Sure, you are." The old man splashed bacanora into another cup. "And I'll thank you not to use that saloon talk in front of my granddaughter."

"Well, old man, I reckon you have me at a disadvantage." Miller laughed as he opened and closed his hands around the shotgun aimed at the old man's belly. "Albeit a small one." He cut his eyes to the girl again. "And I'll bet she's heard worse talk than that."

The girl just stared at him. There was no more fear in her eyes. Her eyes were bold, frank, and her mouth was turned slightly up at the corners.

The old man was about to say something else, but Miller wagged the shotgun at him and said, "Sit down there, and shut up, old man. Drink your busthead. And keep them paws up where I can see 'em." He looked at the girl. "You — Jodi. Can you sew?"

"Of course I can sew," she said. "What do you need sewn?"

"Me."

Miller walked around the table and into

the small parlor area fronting the fire. There was a large, braided rug in there, as well as a rocking chair. He sagged into the rocker, and, holding the shotgun slack across his knees, kicked out of his boots. "Fetch a needle and catgut, and if you're shy, you better avert your eyes. Because I'm gonna get buck naked so I can dry out in front of this nice fire here. Damn, it's a nice one, too. Lordy, that heat feels good!"

"You can't get naked in here!" the old man roared.

"And bring me a blanket," Miller said as the girl climbed the stairs to the loft. "Make that two!"

"She ain't your slave," the old man scolded from the table, where he was sitting now and slowly packing his pipe. "And I done told you to keep your clothes on, you owl-hoot!"

"Ah, shit — I know who you are." Miller was standing and unbuttoning his shirt. "Sure enough — this is the Superstition Station, so you gotta be Old Man Zimmerman. Sure enough, I heard of you." He glanced at the loft where the girl was moving around and the cat was still staring down at Miller. "Heard of your grand-daughter, too."

"So you have," the old man said, glaring

over his pipe at the outlaw, who shucked out of his shirt and tossed it down in front of the fire.

Miller glanced at the pick on the table. The girl appeared to have been greasing a pair of old saddlebags, as well, and also working on a pack frame.

"You two go off in the desert, I hear," Miller said, thoughtful. "Up into the Superstitions."

"So what?"

"You lookin' for that old mine?" Miller grinned. "That old mine that that old Dutchman from Phoenix supposedly found?" His grin broadened. "The lost Peralta diggin's?"

"Like I said," the old man snarled, scratching a match to life atop the table and touching it to the bowl of his porcelain-bowled meerschaum. "So what if we do? Look around. You'll see we ain't found nothin'. Nothin' but coyotes, Apaches, and rattlesnakes."

"No, but I'll bet you two know them mountains like the backs of your hands by now." Miller shoved his denims down to his knees and sat back down in the rocking chair. He looked at the girl moving down the stairs with a wicker sewing kit hooked over one arm. "Sure enough — I bet you two know every nook and cranny of that country."

"Jodi, look away, fer chrissakes!" the old man bellowed, choking on pipe smoke. "Can't you see this crazy owlhoot's half *nek-kid*?!" His anger appeared to dwindle quickly as another thought dawned on him.

He turned to Miller. "Say, who in the hell's doggin' you, anyways?"

CHAPTER 6
THE MEANEST SON OF A BITCH IN THE TERRITORY

The next dawn, Miller opened his eyes in the Zimmerman cabin's loft, and saw a wildcat staring at him devilishly, ready to pounce.

"Holy shit!" the outlaw screamed, and reached toward where he usually positioned his pistol when he bedded down either outside or indoors.

But the gun wasn't there. Instead, he grabbed a handful of Miss Jodi Zimmerman's hair, causing the girl to groan and lift her head from her pillow.

"What the hell?" the girl complained, glancing over her bare right shoulder at him.

Miller rose to a half-sitting position, drawing the sheet up protectively against his chest while he flailed his right hand for his pistol and stared at the beast that didn't seem so ready to pounce, after all. Jodi's bobcat, Claws, lounged atop the mirrored dresser off the foot of the brass bed that took up most of the space in the cluttered loft.

The cat stared at the outlaw with a vague, almost bored interest, slowly blinking its copper eyes. It curled its tail and flicked it and then gave a mewl as it climbed to its feet, humping its back as it stretched.

It dropped over the side of the dresser to land on the floor and give another, louder mewl.

Miller remembered that he'd laid Old Man Zimmerman's shotgun on the floor beside the bed, and he turned over too quickly, reaching for it. The stitches the girl had sewn his wound closed with barked and showed their own nasty fangs, chewing into him, and he forestalled the effort and clutched his side with a yelp.

"Turn your horns in," the girl said in a sleep-raspy voice. "It's just Claws." She glanced toward the cottonwood rail running along the edge of the loft, and yelled, "Old man, let Claws out!"

Miller lay back against his pillow, clutching his side. The girl had sewed it up tight as a drum. It didn't appear to have bled at all last night. And generally the wound felt better. He probably owed that to all the Mexican busthead he'd drunk the night before, though the dull pain in his head was no doubt the cost.

Miller smacked his lips together — his mouth tasted like a tarantula had crawled inside and died under his tongue — and said, "The old man ain't gonna be movin' around too much this mornin'."

He chuckled dryly.

The girl sat up and swept her tangled hair out of her face. She gave a grunt as she remembered that Miller had ordered her to tie old Zimmerman to his rocking chair before she and Miller had sauntered up to the loft together. She gave her own dry chuckle and said, "I was wonderin' why it was so quiet down there."

She threw the sheet off her naked body and dropped her long legs to the floor. Miller reached for her but she batted his hand away. "I gotta let Claws out, get a fire goin'." She gave him a sultry glare over her shoulder. "Less'n you don't want breakfast."

Miller raked his cheek brusquely against her right arm. "You behave yourself down there. Keep that old devil tied to his chair and remember I got his shotgun."

"You're a tough one, ain't ya?"

The girl spread her hand across his unshaven face, and pushed his head back against his pillow. Then she rose and dropped a cotton nightshirt over her head.

It hung down to just below her knees. She swept her hair back behind her head, yawned, and descended the loft stairs to the main room.

"Throw some grub into a cavy sack while you're at it!" Miller yelled. "We're gonna need food on the trail!"

"What trail?" she said from the main room, padding toward the door.

"The trail to Superstition," Miller said, suddenly realizing, by the buttery light angling through the loft's single, sashed window, that it was way past dawn and he had to get up and get moving before Hawk showed. Miller had no doubt he would.

The rogue lawman was known for not leaving a trail until his efforts had paid off in the form of dead men. Miller would have to fight eventually, but first he'd lead Hawk into unfamiliar territory. Into *rugged* territory. And then, when he had the high ground and the upper hand, Pima Miller would rid the frontier once and for all of the loco, upside-down lawman.

And he'd also pull down the hefty bounty he'd heard had piled up on the rogue lawman's head.

Miller rose and stumbled naked over to the dresser and threw back half a jug of stale water. He followed it up with what was left in the bacanora jug, and then picked up the shotgun, hooked his pistol belt over his shoulder, and stumbled downstairs, his knees stiff as half-set mortar from his cold swim in the arroyo. The old man sat in the rocking chair on the other side of the hearth.

He was awake, his red-rimmed, red-veined eyes open, wrists tied behind his back, ankles lashed together. He'd been gagged with a polka-dotted blue neckerchief. He sat rock-still, glowering up at Miller from beneath his shaggy brows.

Miller chuckled at him as the outlaw gathered his clothes from where he'd hung them from chair backs in front of the now-cold fire. Miller dressed and then, as the girl prepared breakfast in sullen silence, he cleaned his pistol, found a couple of boxes of .44 shells and an old-model Winchester rifle, and cleaned and loaded that, too.

Neither Miller nor the girl said anything. Of course the old man did not because Miller kept him gagged. The old man sat facing the hearth but kept his eyes rolled toward Miller in stony, hateful silence.

When Miller and Jodi had eaten, Miller told her to prepare food for the trail.

"We can't go on no trail with you," Jodi snapped, clearing the table. "We got a stage due today, tomorrow at the latest."

"You just shut up and do as I say or I'll gut-shoot both of you and leave you howlin'!" Miller glanced at the old man. "Besides, who said he was goin'? He'd just slow us down."

He looked at Jodi again. "I've heard you and him been livin' out here, running the station and combin' them mountains yonder for that Peralta gold since you was six years old. Now, I could tell from last night that that was a few years ago."

He laughed through his teeth as he turned to the old man, who started tossing his head and grunting furiously. Miller threw back the last of his coffee, rose from the table, walked over to Zimmerman, and jerked the gag down to his whiskered chin.

"What the hell you want, old man?"

"I gotta take a piss, you sonofabitch!"

Miller cursed and went back to the table. He found a folding knife among the girl's clutter, opened the knife, and held the blade up close against Zimmerman's leathery neck.

"How 'bout if I just slit your throat and put everyone whose ever had to have anything to do with you out of their misery?"

"Go ahead!" the old man barked raspily, lifting his chin to expose his lumpy throat. "I'd just as soon not live no more after what

71

I heard up in the loft last night!"

Jodi laughed at that.

So did Miller.

He untied the old man and kicked him outside to drain his bladder off the stoop. And then he forced old Zimmerman to go on out to the barn and saddle a couple of riding horses, and to outfit them with grub sacks and canteens. He wanted a rifle sheath on one of the mounts, as well.

"They better be the best mounts in your remuda, old man," Miller barked, standing on the stoop and waving his pistol at the old man's back as Zimmerman trudged, bandy-legged and cursing profusely, off to the barn and corral in which several horses milled.

Miller walked out into the soggy, steaming yard and stared nearly straight south, toward the rusty crags forming what looked like a giant Gothic cathedral but which comprised, in fact, Superstition Mountain. It seemed to rest suspended above the misty horizon, the mountain's sheer, three-thousand-foot cliffs, pinnacles, and vertical canyons towering over the saguaro-studded desert.

Miller picked out the slender, finger-shaped peak known as Weaver's Needle. It was near that formation that the old Dutchman's mine was said to reside — formerly the mine of one Don Miguel Peralta.

But Miller cared nothing for the Dutchman's gold. He doubted it even existed. It wasn't called Superstition Mountain for nothing. All the outlaw wanted was to lure Gideon Hawk up there into that devil's maze of clefts, canyons, and washes, and shoot the holy hell out of him.

Miller looked all around the station yard, pocked with many mud puddles amid the snaking fingers of steam rising now as the morning heated up, and then he went back inside to hurry the girl. Twenty minutes later, the old man led the two horses back to the cabin, and Miller and Jodi filled their saddlebags and cavy sacks with trail supplies, including the bacon sandwiches she'd made.

Miller tied the old man up in his rocking chair. There was no reason to gag him. He could yell all he wanted. There likely wouldn't be anyone to hear him for several hours.

"He's gonna catch you, whoever he is doggin' your trail."

"Who is he?" Miller challenged the old man.

"I don't know, but whoever he is, to have Pima Miller pissin' down his leg, he must

73

be good!" Old Man Zimmerman cackled at that, eyes sparking devilishly.

Miller unsheathed his Remy and clicked the hammer back.

"He's a mouthy old bastard," Jodi said. "But if you kill him, you're ridin' alone. Good luck gettin' into those mountains without knowin' the way. Geronimo will find you and cook you slow!"

Miller drew his index finger taut against the Remy's trigger. He could kill the old man and force the girl to show him the way, but she'd likely run him into a box canyon. She was savvy. Easier to let the old man live, he supposed.

Miller turned to her. She was holding a cavy sack over her shoulder.

"Get mounted up!" he yelled, glaring at the old man.

He depressed the Remington's hammer, left the cabin, and drew the door closed behind him.

But he couldn't stand letting the old man live. When they were two hundred yards south of the station, Miller stopped and dragged the girl off her horse. She fought him, cursing, but he finally got her hog-tied. Then he tied her horse's reins to a spindly cottonwood.

"You poison-mean son of a bitch!" she

barked at him, lying belly down on the ground, legs and arms drawn up behind her back. Her pretty face was flushed with fury.

"That's right!" Miller raked out, laughing. "I'm the meanest son of a bitch in the territory!"

He galloped back toward the station yard. The trussed-up girl watched him. From her vantage, Miller was a small, brown silhouette by the time he reached the station. She stared through the fog snakes as he dismounted and leapt onto the porch.

He was out of sight for few seconds before the girl heard the dull crack of the outlaw's pistol.

Jodi stared toward the station yard. She blinked slowly. Her mouth corners rose.

CHAPTER 7
DUST AND BONE

Hawk was up at dawn, lashing two four-foot-long oak branches together with rawhide he'd found in the barn behind Nan-tee's now-vacant shack. He'd soaked the rawhide in a water trough, and now he knelt atop the two branches, where they formed a cross, and tightly wound the wet rawhide around the joint.

He tied the hide and used the back of a shovel blade to hammer the cross into the ground, at the head of Nan-tee's grave, on the far side of a shallow wash flanking the barn. He lowered the shovel, caught his breath, and looked at the mound of rocks.

Odd how he no longer felt anything but a slight, lingering guilt. He was well aware he'd orphaned the little boy, but it had been a mistake he'd declared to himself as honest. The woman's killing had been inadvertent, and he'd done as much as he could to repay Nan-tee for having killed her and orphaning her boy.

Having her buried and marking her grave was as much as he could do. Vivienne had taken the boy to an Apache woman who lived with her father and two children in a hogan-type lodge in the desert west of Spotted Horse.

Hawk said no words over the dead woman. He knew a few, but they refused to be remembered. He'd said them before, and ever since his family had been taken from him, they'd sounded laughably hollow.

He'd tried it again just a few months ago, when he and his blonde sometimes-partner Saradee Jones had visited the two graves outside the town of Crossroads in southern Dakota Territory. Hawk had been wounded in an especially violent shoot-out, and his nearness to his own death had fueled the urge to be near his dead family again. But to Hawk the two graves in that stark cemetery had merely been two depressions in the ground capped with wood fashioned into crosses — home to nothing more substantial than a few shovelfuls of dust and bits of bone.

Those two holes in the ground did not house his family. His family — the love and the laughter and the times he and Jubal had fished a nearby creek together — were gone.

They'd been taken from Hawk and this world by Three-Fingers Ned Meade.

All they were, all they would have been . . . gone.

It was a bone that Hawk could not get out of his craw. Killing Pima Miller wouldn't do it, either. He had no illusions.

But Miller needed killing if for no other reason than a young mother had taken a bullet meant for him. But of course there were many more reasons. Miller was a killer. He'd even killed the sawbones who'd dug Hawk's bullet out of his hide. By hunting him down and killing him, Hawk would feel better.

He would feel, for an hour, maybe an hour and a half — no more than that — *better.*

And then, when the feeling passed, he'd clean and reload his weapons and look for the next man who needed killing.

Or the next woman. Women were not immune to evildoing.

Saradee Jones, for instance. There was likely no worse woman anywhere. And she needed killing. But so far, Hawk hadn't been able to drop the hammer on her. He'd only been able to feast himself on her splendid body while she taunted him for doing so.

One day, however, he would kill her.

Maybe the next time he saw her, in fact.

Footsteps sounded behind Hawk. One hand went to the grips of the silver-plated Russian as he turned. He removed his hand from the gun. Vivienne walked toward him. As she made her way across the wash, she carried a burlap sack in one hand, a steaming stone mug in the other.

She wore her black hair pulled back in an enticingly sloppy French braid. A cream-colored, Mexican-style dress with red embroidering hugged her fine body, buffeting around her brown legs. The dress left her shoulders bare.

The long, pale scar running down the side of her face stood out in the weak morning light.

The grulla, saddled and ready for the trail, Hawk's Henry rifle snugged down in the saddle boot, whickered and turned to the girl, as well, switching its tail.

"Easy, fella," Hawk said, patting the horse's neck. "She's a friend."

"A friend, eh?" Vivienne smiled ironically as she climbed the shallow bank, likely remembering the passion of their previous night's coupling. She held out the coffee and the tied neck of the bag to Hawk. "Food for the trail. Parched corn for your horse. I thought you might like a cup of coffee before you go."

Hawk stared at her, vaguely puzzled.

"I had a feeling I'd find you here," she said.

"Why?"

"Just a feeling."

Hawk took the cup and the grub sack, and sipped the coffee. It was hot and black.

Vivienne folded her arms on her breasts as she looked down at Nan-tee's grave. Then she glanced at him. "Where's your wife?"

"How do you know there was a wife?"

"You look like a killer. Kill like a killer. But last night . . ." Vivienne shrugged a shoulder. "I don't know. You were nice. Gentle. Figure there must be a woman behind that."

"There was."

"And a child?"

Hawk stared over the mug as he sipped the coffee.

"I found a carving — a wooden horse, a black stallion — on the floor in my room. It must have fallen out of your coat pocket. 'Jubal' is written on the bottom." Vivienne paused. "I wrapped it up and put it in the grub sack."

"Obliged. It's my boy's. *Was* my boy's."

"I'm sorry, Gideon. Whatever happened,

80

I'm sorry. I hope you find peace sometime, somewhere . . . despite it all."

"Ain't likely. But I appreciate your sayin' the words, Vivienne. Just the same."

She reached out and slid a finger across the moon-and-star badge pinned upside down to his vest.

"Farewell, Upside-down Lawman. Watch your back. Pima Miller is a sneaky devil. Some say Nan-tee gave him secret Apache powers that make him extra strong, extra hard to kill."

Hawk finished the coffee and handed the cup back to Vivienne. "We'll see."

Hawk tied the grub sack to his saddle horn then stepped into the leather. He did not look back at the woman from the Laughing Lady Saloon as he put the horse into a trot through the chaparral, heading south, the same direction in which Pima Miller had headed.

As Hawk had expected, the storm had washed away most of Miller's sign. But Hawk's own Ute war chief father had taught him how to track long ago, and he'd put those skills to good use, gaining experience during the years he'd worked as a bona fide federal lawman.

He'd honed said skills to a razor's edge

after he'd begun tracking men for his own satisfaction, with a hard heart and the unflappable determination of a religious fanatic. There was probably presently no better tracker on the frontier than Gideon Hawk, excepting possibly one or two Apache trackers now working for the US Army under the supervision of General Crook, or some of the Pima and Maricopa Indians whom John Walker had trained to fight Geronimo's Chiricahuas.

To complement those skills, Hawk was as patient as he was determined, and patience was key when tracking on the lee side of a desert gully washer.

Hawk had last seen Miller heading south, toward the Superstition Mountains that were now in the early morning a gray-green lump on the southern horizon. As Hawk rode through the chaparral, weaving around saguaros, barrel cactus, mesquites, and palo verdes, he saw the remnants of the previous day's rain — the desert caliche and soft clays whipped into small swirls and still-damp, miniature deltas that had eroded any markings left by the killer.

But, still, Hawk found parts of prints on the lee sides of trees and occasional boulders, where the rain had had less direct access to them. He also found several relatively fresh horse apples and even a bit of cloth clinging to a cholla branch — a few threads of blue chambray that had been torn from the same color shirt as the one Miller had been wearing when Hawk had last seen the killer.

By noon, Hawk had progressed only a mile from Spotted Horse, but as Miller's trail was leading almost directly south, he was relatively certain it would continue in that direction, toward the Superstitions whose steep, gray crags continued changing both shape and color along the southern horizon as the sun kited across the sky.

As Hawk rode and continued picking up small signs of his quarry's passing, he put himself in the mind of Miller. The killer had ridden through here during a downpour. He'd also been wounded. Those two things had likely made him a desperate man. One who had likely not been sure that Hawk hadn't been following him.

Doubtless, the man wouldn't have cared much about which direction he was riding. He'd likely given his horse its head and just hung on, hoping to find some place in which he could cower from the lightning, thunder, and hammering rain.

Since he'd been heading south, he'd probably continued heading south.

Hawk continued his slow ride, scanning the ground as well as the flora around him, throughout most of the afternoon, wanting to make sure he was still on Miller's trail. He didn't care if it took him a week to ride five miles. As long as he was still on Miller's trail, he'd eventually catch up to the man and kill him.

He hoped Miller wouldn't die from his bullet wound before the rogue lawman could run him down. He wanted the satisfaction of being the last person the killer saw before he was sent to hell on the burning, gunpowder wings of a .44 slug.

Hawk thought the man who'd left his dead woman — killed with a bullet meant for him — and his small child behind while he'd fled into the night, thinking only of himself, deserved nothing less.

He reached a broad, deep arroyo in the early afternoon, when the distant mountains were relieved by dense shadow, the northwestern rock faces tinged yellow and salmon. Hawk stared down at the cut before him. The water, which was the color of creamed coffee, had receded halfway down the steep banks. Last night, however, it had to have been a veritable millrace.

Hawk looked around, wondering if Miller had made it across or had headed either east or west along the bank. He considered following the arroyo in both directions, but if he remembered right, the Butterfield Company had a stage route running nearby. Miller might have known about the trail and at least tried to head for it. Hawk would check the trail out first, and the first relay station he came to.

Someone might have spotted the wounded killer.

Hawk's grulla mustang crossed the arroyo easily, though it had some trouble climbing the steep opposite bank that was slick with still-wet clay. The horse's hooves slipped, and as it fought for traction, the mustang's lungs wheezed like a blacksmith's bellows.

At the top of the bank, Hawk stopped the horse, resting him, and looked around.

To his right, a saguaro leaned out over the wash. The night before, the lip of the wash had eroded enough to uproot the cactus. Now, among the bone-colored roots that had been partially torn out of the ground, something glistened in the afternoon sunshine.

Something Miller had left behind? Possibly a canteen?

Hawk swung down from the saddle, dropped to a knee beside the saguaro, reached through the roots, and took hold of the object.

He saw right away that whatever it was couldn't have belonged to Miller, for it was too deeply entangled in the saguaro's roots. However, curiosity urged him to disentangle the roots until he was holding before him a badly dented and rusted Spanish-style helmet from which the rain had washed away some of the mud. Despite the weathering, Hawk recognized the headgear by its flat, narrow brim and the high crest, like a rooster's comb, running from front to back.

Only one cheek guard clung to it. The other was likely entangled deeper in the root ball, or maybe it had long ago been blown or washed away in rains similar to that which had ravaged this desert the night before.

Hawk ran his hands along the helmet's flaking metal brim. Finding these ancient artifacts always gave him a chill. They reminded him how small and insignificant he was. Even how small and insignificant his *misery* was — merely one clipped scream among the barrage of screams and long, keening wails that comprised all of human life on earth from the first mortal forward.

He peered through the bristling chaparral toward the castle-like Superstitions rising in the south. He'd heard that a rich Mexican whose family had owned a sprawling rancho had come north on a gold-scouting expedition about forty years ago. Don Miguel Peralta had been chasing a legend that the Apaches had told Coronado about a vein of almost pure gold in the high, rugged range two hundred miles north of what is now the US–Mexico border.

Discovering that the vein was more than mere legend — that the nearly pure gold did, in fact, exist — Peralta recruited several hundred peons to work his "Sombrero Mine" deep inside the Superstitions, and over the next three years he shipped home by pack train millions of pesos' worth of nearly pure gold concentrate.

Hawk looked down at the helmet in his hands.

Could he be holding the headgear of one of Coronado's men who, exploring this country three hundred years ago, first became privy to the Apache story of almost-pure gold? The gold that Don Peralta mined later, before the Civil War, and ended up selling his life to the Apaches for?

Dust and bone . . .

Hawk heard a scream. Loud and shrill, it came from inside his own head. It was the scream of his wife when Linda learned that their boy, Jubal, had been taken off the school playground and hanged by Three-Fingers Ned Meade.

Hawk tossed the helmet aside, swung up onto the grulla's back, and continued south toward the stage road and, he hoped, more sign that he was on the trail of Pima Miller.

The wind wasn't blowing, but the rogue lawman could smell blood on the breeze . . .

CHAPTER 8
THE STAGE FROM FLAGSTAFF

The old man sat back in his rocking chair, both open eyes rolled up and slightly off-center as though he were staring at the bullet hole in his forehead.

Blood trickled from the hole past the corner of his left eye and along his nose to pool in the mustache of his blue-white Vandyke beard. His arms had been tied behind him to the spools at the back of the chair, and his ankles were bound. His lower jaw sagged, upper lips stretched back from his crooked, yellow teeth in the same snarl he'd likely given his killer.

Extending the cocked Russian in his right hand, Hawk looked around the shack. He didn't have to inspect it to know that no one else was there. A deathly silence filled the place, and dirty dishes were mounded in the dry sink to the right of the range on which were several greasy pots and pans. Flour had been spilled on the table, near a mess of freshly oiled tack and the hide-wrapped handle of a pickax. The flour told Hawk that someone had hastily packed for the trail, and that that person had likely gone with Miller.

That Miller had shot the trussed-up, defenseless old man, there was no doubt in Hawk's mind. A woman had lived here with the old man, for the kitchen, however messy, bespoke a woman's touch. The slight fragrance of lilac water mixed with the smell of man sweat and tobacco in the cabin's hot, pent-up air still humid from the previous night's storm.

Hawk turned and walked out through the cabin's open door. He held the Russian down along his leg as he moved off the porch and walked around the yard, closely inspecting the ground. He stopped near the windmill and stared south.

Then he holstered the hog leg, stepped up onto the grulla's back, and trotted on out of the yard, following an oft-used wagon trail that appeared to meander over the low benches in the direction of the Superstitions standing tall now on the horizon, orange and pink in the light of the falling sun.

Fifteen minutes later, content that he had Miller's trail — two shod horses heading south toward the mountains — Hawk returned to the yard and unsaddled his mount in the barn. He took great care with the grulla, watering and graining the mount and then slowly, thoroughly wiping him down with an old feed sack and then currying him and cleaning out his hooves. The horse had picked up a few pebbles and cactus thorns, and they had to be tended to prevent trouble as he trailed Miller.

Hawk was well aware that without his horse, the hunt would be over. And once he left the stage station and headed up into the Superstitions, his horse would be even more essential. If the mustang went down, Hawk's own life would be over.

And Pima Miller would ride free with his hostage.

If the girl or woman was, indeed, a hostage. Hawk had seen no signs of a struggle, so he couldn't be sure. He'd heard that Miller held a devilish attraction for women, and any girl living alone out here with the now-deceased old man would probably be susceptible to the killer's charms.

Miller might be using her as a guide rather than a hostage. The cabin was filled with mining implements, as was the barn and tack room, which meant that the old man and possibly the girl were at least part-time prospectors, and likely knew the mountains well.

By the time Hawk had finished tending his own horse and feeding and watering the stage horses and three burros and headed back to the cabin, the sun had slid down behind the far western ridges that were silhouetted black against it. He saw no reason to continue after Miller that day.

Tomorrow would be soon enough. It would likely rain tonight, as already more monsoon clouds were building in the southwest, but Miller would no doubt continue to follow the well-worn trail leading south of the station yard.

Obviously, he was intending on either hiding in the mountains until his trail grew cold, or on leading his hunter into the high crags, isolating him and bushwhacking him from the ample cover of that wild country. Or maybe he intended to work through them to the south. Hawk knew that the outlaw's home territory was the desert around Tucson. He'd acquired his nickname, Pima, from having been married to a Pima girl for a time, when he'd been hauling freight to Arizona cavalry outposts in the years following the war.

That had been before he'd turned to sundry, more nefarious, means of making his living . . .

Back in the shack, Hawk built a fire in the range and untied the old man from the rocking chair. Using picks and shovels from the cabin, Hawk buried the old man behind the shack, first wrapping his body in a tattered quilt. He had to rush the job because of the storm's approach, with drumming thunder and a chill, rising breeze, but he was content that he'd ensconced the old man's body safely from the predators.

He brewed coffee on the cabin's range and sipped it outside on the porch, watching the rain come down, feeling refreshed by the chill, damp breeze. Later, he ate one of the two remaining burritos that Vivienne had made, with a pickled chili pepper she'd also packed. For dessert he sipped tequila from the small stone bottle she'd wrapped in heavy burlap, fingering the wooden stallion his boy had carved only a few days before he'd died . . .

The storm didn't last half as long as the one the night before, and Hawk was glad. It would make following Miller easier. The thunder rumbled for nearly an hour after the brunt of the storm, lightning flashing in the northeast.

The air was fresh and cool, perfumed by

the desert.

Hawk slept in one of the beds in the curtained-off area of the cabin reserved for overnight passengers. He slept well, knowing that he was on a warm trail, confident that he would kill another killer soon.

That morning, just after dawn, he drank coffee and ate his last burrito and pickled chili pepper outside on the porch again. He'd saddled the grulla and tied the horse to the hitch rack fronting the cabin. As Hawk finished the burrito and washed the last bite down with another swallow of coffee, the grulla gave its tail a hard switch and turned its head to peer toward the trail curving out of the desert.

Its ears twitched as it stood, tensely staring toward the north.

Slowly, Hawk leaned forward and set his plate and cup on the porch rail. Then he reached behind him for the Henry he'd leaned against the shack. He pumped a live round in the chamber, off-cocked the hammer, and rested the rifle across his thighs.

Presently, a man's yell, muffled by distance, pierced the morning quiet and stillness. The faint din of galloping hooves followed, gradually growing louder. Many sets of hooves. As the man's yells continued, punctuated with what sounded like the pops of a small-caliber pistol but which Hawk recognized as a blacksnake being snapped over a team's back, Hawk eased his grip on the rifle.

The yells were those of a jehu haranguing his team.

A stage was approaching from the north.

Hawk sat back in the chair and waited, hearing the commotion growing louder until the stage came into view along the trail, the six horses lunging forward against their collars, the jehu sitting on the right side of the driver's box, whistling now more than yelling.

The shotgun messenger sat to the driver's left, cradling the sawed-off, double-bore coach gun in his arms. As the stage drew near, the jehu — a stocky man in a high-crowned, salt-encrusted cream hat and wearing a red neckerchief with white polka dots up high across his mouth and nose — eased back on the ribbons he was deftly plying in his gloved hands. Above his hands, thick leather gauntlets ringed his forearms.

The team and its trailing coach thundered into the yard. It came around the far side of the windmill and stock tank, and the jehu leaned back in the seat, pressing his boots against the dashboard, as he hauled back on the reins. The shotgun messenger was cautiously eyeing Hawk still sitting on the stage station's front stoop. The shotgun rider lowered his neckerchief, and Hawk saw that a wad of chaw was bulging his left cheek.

When the driver had the team stopped, he ripped his own neckerchief down from his nose and yelled, *"Zimmerman!"* He cast his incredulous gaze from Hawk to the closed station house door and then back toward the barn and pole corral. *"Jodi! Zimmerman! Stage from Flagstaff!"*

Hawk said, "They're not here."

He glanced through the door of the coach sitting about thirty feet straight in front of him. He thought there were four or five passengers jostling around inside the Concorde, preparing to de-stage. A woman was coughing and waving a hand in front of her face as though to clear the dust roiling around inside the cramped confines.

Hawk's gaze caught on the flash of something shiny.

A badge, perhaps?

"Where are they?" the shotgun messenger asked Hawk, looking over the driver who was just then setting the brake and spitting dust from his lips.

Hawk stared through the window of the stage door. Sure enough, one of the passengers wore a badge. From Hawk's position, it looked like the moon-and-star badge of a federal.

"Did you hear me, mister?" the bellicose shotgun messenger said, scowling at Hawk. "Where's Jodi and the old man?"

Hawk said, "The old man's dead. Buried behind the station house. Jodi — does that happen to be a male or a female?"

The driver was glowering at Hawk, apparently not certain he'd heard correctly. "Female! What's this about Zimmerman?"

"Dead," Hawk said.

The driver and the shotgun messenger glanced at each other skeptically. Then they both started to climb down off their perch.

At the same time, the stage's near door opened, and a tall man in a three-piece suit so dusty that it appeared gray stepped down into the yard. A badge was pinned to his wool vest. He cast Hawk a dark, critical stare and then he turned to help down from the stage a middle-aged woman in a green traveling frock and small straw hat trimmed with fake berries and flowers.

The next man out, also middle-aged and wearing a shabby suit and wool shirt with attached collar, appeared to be the woman's husband. His corduroy trousers were patched at the knees. The man and the woman stepped to one side, looking around

97

with the typically harried, disoriented expressions of stage travelers — especially those who'd likely been held up on account of the weather. The man beat his bowler hat against his leg, causing more dust to billow.

As the lawman continued to regard Hawk skeptically, his eyes flicking between the Henry resting across Hawk's knees, and Hawk's face, two more men climbed heavily, wearily down from the stage behind him. These two were dressed similarly to the first man, and they also wore deputy US marshal's badges. Ever so slightly and slowly, Hawk used his left middle finger and the heel of that hand to slide his coat across his own upside-down badge, concealing it.

He didn't know if the others had noticed. He hoped not. He was not in the business of killing lawmen. Unless they got in his way.

Then they were as fair game as men like Pima Miller.

The stocky driver strode up the porch steps, batting his own hat against his thigh, and said, "You pullin' some kinda funny, mister?"

"About what?"

"About Zimmerman bein' dead?"

"Nope," Hawk said. "I never joke about death. I found him in there yesterday, tied to his rocking chair. Someone had drilled a bullet through his forehead. He was getting cold and starting to swell, so I buried him."

The driver tripped the latch, opened the door, and stepped inside, yelling, *"Zimmerman?"* He waited. "Miss Jodi?"

"I told you," Hawk said, gaining his feet. "He's around back."

The driver stepped back out of the station house. He and the shotgun messenger shared a look, and then the driver hurried back down the porch steps and walked swiftly around the corner of the cabin, heading for the rear. The shotgun messenger gave Hawk an owly look as he rested his shotgun on his shoulder, spat a dark stream of chaw onto a prickly pear, and followed the older man toward the back of the cabin.

The lawmen all looked at each other, and then two followed the jehu and the shotgun messenger around the cabin, while the third lawman and the two civilian passengers stood regarding Hawk skeptically in the morning's dwindling shadows.

Hawk stepped down off the porch. Heading for his horse, he glanced at the middle-aged man and woman, and said, "There's coffee inside."

The man and the woman both glanced expectantly at the deputy US marshal. The federal canted his head toward the station house. He waited until the couple was inside, and then he said, "Hold on, friend."

He stepped toward Hawk, his fingers in the pockets of his butternut wool vest from which a gold-washed watch chain dangled.

He was tall and lean, fair of skin and sunburned at the nubs of his cheeks. His long, slender nose was peeling. Hawk guessed he was in his early thirties. Curly blond hair hung down beneath the flat brim of his coffee-colored Stetson, which boasted a band of rattlesnake skin.

His mouth was long and thin beneath a dragoon-style mustache. His relatively smooth cheeks showed a day-old trace of beard stubble to which dust clung. He carried himself with an air of self-importance as he sauntered toward Hawk, and stopped just off the grulla's right hip.

Hawk was standing on the horse's left side, resting his rifle across the seat of his saddle and then reaching down to tie the latigo strap beneath the horse's belly.

"If what you say is true, friend," the lawman said with a taut smile, "then you're gonna need to hang around and answer a few questions."

"I'm not your friend," Hawk said, pulling the end of the latigo through the saddle's D ring. "And I don't like it when folks get too friendly."

"You said Old Man Zimmerman was dead, friend. And I, bein' a federal lawman an' all, would like to know who killed him."

"Pima Miller killed him. But, again" — Hawk smiled at him over his saddle — "I'm not your *friend.*"

The lawman frowned. "Miller's who we're after. Chief marshal sent us down from Prescott. Miller and his gang robbed the bank in Kingman and are said to be meeting up with the rest of their gang somewhere south of Phoenix."

"No shit?"

"How do you know Miller killed Zimmerman?"

"I just know."

"Hold on, friend!"

The federal walked around the rear of the grulla. Hawk had turned out his left stirrup and was preparing to toe it and mount, when the federal lawman grabbed Hawk's arm. As Hawk turned to face him, the lawman's eyes dropped. Hawk followed the man's glance to Hawk's upside-down badge, which his coat had opened to reveal.

The lawman slowly lifted his chin. When his eyes finally met Hawk's, his brows were beetled with incredulity. "What the . . . ?"

Hawk heard the voices of the other lawmen as they strode back toward the yard from the cabin's rear.

"Let it go, friend," Hawk said, his lips quirking a frigid smile beneath his brushy mustache. "Just let it go."

The lawman's disbelieving gaze flicked from the badge again to Hawk's emerald-hard eyes. "You're . . ."

"They don't have to know," Hawk said mildly. "If they do know, it ain't gonna go well. You know that. You'll just be three dead men with no yesterday, no tomorrow."

Hawk held the lawman's gaze. The man's lower jaw sagged. His eyes were dark with fear, frustration.

"Step away. Be our secret. You boys just keep ridin' on down to Phoenix in the stagecoach there, and you see about Miller and his gang down there . . . and you just think about how you might have died today but didn't because you were smart enough to keep your mouth shut."

"There's a grave back there, sure enough," said one of the other two lawmen as they both rounded the cabin's far front corner. He stopped and nodded toward Hawk. "Have you checked him out, Alvin?"

Alvin stared uncertainly at Hawk. And then he took one step back, saying haltingly,

"Yeah, I checked him out. He seen Miller in the area." He took another step straight back away from Hawk, the grulla between Hawk and the other two lawmen now approaching, the jehu and shotgun messenger behind them.

"He thinks Miller and his bunch is headed for Phoenix . . . just like we thought," Alvin said.

"What about Miss Jodi?" This from the jehu, who'd stopped with the other men near the porch steps.

"I figure they must have taken her," Hawk said, sliding his coat closed and stepping into the leather. He rested his Henry across his saddlebow and backed the grulla away from the hitch rack.

He smiled at Alvin, nodded to the other lawmen and the jehu and shotgun rider, and then swung the grulla around the cabin and put it into a jog across the yard, heading south toward the trail he'd scouted the evening before. For a time, he could hear the lawmen talking behind him. He hoped Alvin kept his mouth shut.

Hawk didn't want to kill lawmen, though he knew from experience that many were no better than the men they were paid to hunt. Some were worse.

Still, he didn't want to kill the lawmen

from Prescott.

But if they trailed him, tried to impede him, he would blow them all to hell.

Chapter 9
Deadly Companion

Miller reined his brindle bay to a halt under a lip of rock that rose out of the canyon floor like a shark's fin, and glanced behind him. He could see no movement down toward the broad neck of the canyon they'd been riding through for the past hour, so he glanced at the girl riding off his left stirrup.

"Get down and start a fire. We'll rest the horses and have lunch here."

"I'm gonna have to gather wood for that fire," Jodi said, climbing off the back of her Morgan mare. "Sure you trust I won't skin off on ya?"

She cast him a devilish grin over her shoulder.

"You stay away from that horse while you're gatherin' that wood, and you stay where I can see you. You try to run off, I'll —"

"Yeah, I know," Jodi said, tying the Morgan to an ironwood shrub in the shade of the shark's fin. "You'll run me down and tan my bare ass and then you'll hobble me and I'll ride belly down over my mare's back for the rest of our wonderful time together."

She snickered as she kicked a chunk of ironwood free of the ground, and then stooped to pick it up.

"Think it's funny, do you?" Miller snarled. "You'll see how funny it is if you try to run out on me."

He reined the bay around and rode back down the old Indian trail they'd been following into the mountains. The trail climbed a low bench overlooking the canyon mouth. Several yards from the top of the bench, Miller stopped the bay, fished old Zimmerman's spyglass out of his saddlebags, and then got down and crawled to the lip of the bench.

He telescoped the glass and stared off across the desert toward the stage station that was lost in the heat haze of the northwestern horizon. All that he could see were low, rocky bluffs, hogbacks, swales and mesas sprinkled liberally with palo verdes, saguaros, mesquites, and clay-colored rock.

Miller carefully scrutinized the desert flanking him. From time to time he glanced over his shoulder at the girl, who appeared to be dutifully gathering wood and building a fire. As the outlaw studied a low mesa rising in the northeast, movement caught his eye closer in and on his right. His heart hiccupping, he jerked the spyglass in that direction, followed a gray-brown blur of movement until the object stopped atop a flat rock.

Miller stared through the glass, adjusting the focus.

His heartbeat slowed. The outlaw shaped a wry smile. What he was looking at was none other than the girl's bobcat, Claws, who just now leaped down off the rock to lie in a wedge of shade leaning out from it.

The bobcat stared toward Miller, flicking its bobbed tail.

Miller chuckled. Then he reduced the spyglass, slipped it back into its deerskin poke, rose, and tramped down the slope to his horse. He looked back toward their noon camp. The girl had a small fire going, thin tendrils of gray smoke rising from orange flames. She was on one knee, pouring water from a canteen into a small, black coffeepot.

She glanced over her shoulder at Miller. He was too far away to see her face clearly, but he'd gotten to know her well enough to know she was smirking. Something inside him wanted to wipe that smirk off her face, to bring her to heel like a dog. He didn't care for women thinking they were better than him.

But he needed her to get him through the mountains after he bushwhacked Hawk, so he had to keep his temper on a short leash. Besides, he couldn't beat her up too badly. He needed her in good health to quell his natural male desires.

"You don't care one bit that I killed the old man, do you?" Miller asked her when he'd ridden over to the fire. He'd dismounted and was loosening the bay's latigo strap, so the horse could rest easy.

She was sitting on a rock near the fire, leaning forward, elbows on her knees, gloved hands together. She was giving him that look again. That look like she knew more than he did about something, or that she was better than he was.

Or maybe she found him funny to look at. He knew he wasn't the best-looking gent, but he had a way with women, and he'd had none too few, neither. And that kid he'd left at Nan-tee's wasn't the only son he'd sired, neither.

When she didn't say anything but merely continued to give him that faintly jeering look through those bold, hazel eyes of hers, he said, "What in the hell you lookin' at, goddamnit? What you thinkin' about?"

She hiked a shoulder and glanced away. "I'm just thinkin'."

"Why don't you answer my question?"

"What question?"

"Old Zimmerman. Your grand*paw*!"

"Oh, him," she said, shrugging again and then lifting her boot toes and staring down at them. "Well, he's dead now and I never really cared for him. The old bastard was in my way, if you want the truth. So, you killed him. You shouldn't have, but you did. I didn't have no part in it, and there wasn't nothin' I could do to stop you, so I reckon I got a good story for old Saint Pete when I see him. About *that,* anyways."

Miller stared at her, incredulous. Then he chuckled and dug his horse's feed sack out of a saddlebag pouch. "You're a piece of work, girl. Yes, ma'am, you purely are!"

When he'd hung a feed bag of oats over the bay's ears, he started to sit down on a rock near the girl. He stopped when the stitches in his wound pulled, feeling that rat gnawing on him again. Then he eased himself down on the rock, pressing a hand over the wound and wincing.

"Don't let the coffee boil over," the girl said, rising and heading off into the brush on the far side of the horses.

"Where the hell you goin'?"

She disappeared among some boulders. He could hear her thrashing around, grunting softly. When the coffeepot started to boil, Miller used a swatch of burlap to remove it from the flames.

He dumped a handful of ground Arbuckle's into the water, let it return to a boil and then removed it from the flames again, setting the hissing pot on a rock to the right of the fire. Miller jerked his head up when the girl strode back into their little camp. She had a pocket knife in her right hand and a mess of what looked like cactus pulp in the other.

"Hey, where'd you get that knife?" Miller asked, scowling at the open blade in her hand.

"Slipped it into my boot before we left the station. Figured it might come in handy. Don't get your shorts in a twist. Open your shirt and I'll smear this prickly-pear pulp on those stitches. It'll take some of the pain away and keep it from festering."

Miller knew the remedy, as he'd been married to a Pima girl and lived among her family for a year. Those people could make a meal out of a single cholla branch. Keeping his eyes on the barlow knife in Jodi's hand, Miller jerked his shirttails out of his jeans, and pulled the shirt up to expose the wound she'd stitched closed. The wound appeared relatively clean, but some yellow fluid was leaking out through the seam in his puckered skin, between the stitches that looked like clipped cat whiskers.

As Jodi used her finger to smear the pulp into the wound, Miller sucked a sharp breath through his teeth.

"Easy!"

"Stop your caterwauling."

When she'd coated the wound with the cactus pulp, Jody brushed the excess on her trouser leg.

"I'll take that," Miller said, and reached for the knife.

She pulled it away and, grinning, sort of did a two-step around the fire before bending over and sliding the barlow back into the well of her right boot. "I haven't stuck you so far, have I?"

"You little bitch."

"Chicken shit!"

Jodi laughed and then sauntered back over to the coffeepot.

She added cold water to settle the grounds then poured them each a cup while Miller scowled at her, knowing he'd be sleeping even lighter at night than he usually did. He'd be wondering if she was going to slip the blade of that knife between his ribs.

Deciding he'd deal with the knife later, he accepted a cup of steaming coffee from her, sat on a rock, and stared along their back trail.

Jodi warmed some beans and rabbit meat in a small skillet, and while they ate their burritos around the fire, she said, "Who's behind you, killer?"

Miller had been chewing and staring off toward the mouth of the canyon again. He looked at her, swallowed, sipped his coffee, and grunted, "What?"

Sitting on a rock on the far side of the fire, the girl took a big bite of her burrito and said around the unladylike mouthful, "You're nervous as a doe with a newborn fawn. What wolf you got nippin' at your hocks, killer?"

"Stop callin' me killer or I'll backhand you."

She laughed and shook a lock of her gold-blonde hair out of her eye. "Who's doggin' your trail?"

He didn't like her mocking tone. He was starting to think he should have killed her when he'd killed the old man. Trouble was, he didn't know the Superstitions. He needed a guide.

"What's it to you?"

"Well, if he's doggin' your trail, he's doggin' mine, right?"

"Fella called Hawk." Miller turned his head to stare back down the canyon. "The *rogue lawman,* they call him."

"No kiddin'?" Jodi pitched her voice with pleasant surprise, which also riled Miller. "I've heard of him." She chewed another bite of her burrito and then chuckled again as she said, "What'd you do to get him on your trail?"

"None of your business."

"Where we headin' — you figure that might be my business?"

Miller turned to her. He chewed and sipped his coffee for a time and then he ran his sleeve across his mouth and drooping mustaches and said, "I want you to take me to high ground. Maybe a canyon like this one, but higher up in the mountains. Some place good to set a bushwhack."

"You're gonna kill him? This *rogue lawman?*"

"Yeah, I'm gonna kill him."

"From bushwhack?"

Miller's ears warmed with anger. He glared at her, chewing, and then he swallowed and pointed at her with what remained of his burrito. "You get that tone out of your voice. I don't like it."

"You can threaten me all you want, Pima,"

the girl said saucily. "But if you don't treat me right, I'm liable to lead you into a box canyon, let that rogue lawman fella ride right up on ya. Geronimo hides out from the army up around Weaver's Needle, but I know how to work around him — when I *want* to. Hell, I could lead you into a nest of diamondbacks. Plenty of those out here, and I know where more than a few of 'em are. A prospector named Dunleavy dug into one o' them nests, started screamin' somethin' awful. About six baby rattlers little bigger than this finger was clingin' to his arms. One dug its fangs into his *cheek*!"

She laughed and shook her head. "He was dead in an hour, but let me tell you — that was one hell of a long, loud hour, if you get my drift!"

"You done?"

"What's that?"

"Yappin'. You done?"

Jodi brushed her hand across her mouth, shook her hair back from her head. "Oh, be a sport. I'm just funnin' with ya. I'll help you out . . . as long as you tell me what's next after this."

"What do you mean — what's next?"

"What're you gonna do after you kill this *rogue lawman*?"

"I'm gonna have you lead me out of the

114

mountains to the south. Then, you're clear. You can go back to the station, and I'll head for Mexico."

Jodi swallowed the last of her burrito and curled her upper lip at Miller. "And then you'll work back north and retrieve the money you took out of the Kingman bank."

Miller chuckled dryly. "We didn't get more than a few hundred dollars out of that bank. We hid the money along the trail. Too little to risk goin' back for. Don't worry." Miller grinned, happy to think she thought he might have the upper hand on her for a change. "I ain't holdin' out on ya. I'm broke. All I got is the shirt on my back and my gun, and that's about all."

Jodi considered that for a time. She sipped her coffee. "I might have an idea."

Miller had turned to stare back down the canyon again. Now he looked back at Jodi, whose eyes were wide and grave and missing their customary mockery. "What idea?"

"Just an idea. I'll tell you more after you back shoot this *rogue lawman* fella."

"I didn't say I was gonna back shoot him!"

"Back shoot, bushwhack. Same difference."

Miller's dark eyes glinted angrily. "You know — I was just startin' to think I might could like you."

"Easy, killer." Jodi tossed her cup down, rose from her rock, and walked around the fire. She stopped before Miller and thrust her shoulders back. Her pointed breasts jutted behind her shirt. "You be nice to me, I'll be nice to you."

Giving a smoky smile, she knelt down between his spread knees and reached for the buckle of his cartridge belt.

CHAPTER 10
"DRAG THAT SOGGY BOOT BACK NORTH AND LIVE TO PISS ANOTHER DAY, FRIEND!"

Deputy US Marshal Whit Chaney eased his chestnut around a bend in the wall of the canyon he and his two partners had been following throughout the day, and jerked back on the horse's reins. He frowned as he stared ahead, not liking what he was seeing.

Not liking what he was seeing at all.

The ground rose sharply about seventy yards ahead. A broad jumble of black volcanic rock studded with desert flora appeared to block the trail. From his vantage, he could see no way through it.

Had the man they'd been tracking led them into a box canyon?

He turned to his partners.

The tall, blond-headed Alvin Teagarden rode a buckskin on a parallel course about fifty yards to Chaney's left, on the other side of a dry arroyo that ran down through the canyon's center. Ralph "Hooch" Mortimer rode his dapple-gray nearest Chaney, along a game trail following the arroyo's near side. Both men had seen Chaney stop, because they too had halted their horses and were looking at him warily, apparently wondering what had spooked him.

Chaney lifted his chin toward the steep hill of jumbled rock and tangled cacti ahead of him. And then he looked down at the trail in front of his horse. About twenty yards back, he'd lost sight of the shod hoofprints he'd been following. He saw no sign of them here, either.

Those two troubling facts — the steep wall of boulders ahead of him and the sudden disappearance of the rogue lawman's sign — made Chaney's heart skip. As were most lawmen throughout the frontier, Chaney was well aware of Gideon Hawk's reputation. The man hunted bad men mercilessly. But he showed the same lack of mercy to any lawman who stood between Hawk and his prey.

And he was very, very shrewd.

Shrewd and merciless.

Bad combination.

Chaney looked toward his two compatriots once more, and raised a waylaying hand. Then he stepped down from the chestnut's back, tied the reins to a low shrub, and, slowly and quietly levering a live cartridge

118

into his carbine's action, began walking forward.

He moved one careful step at a time, looking all around him, up and down the gradual, rocky ridges sloping toward the canyon on both sides. He followed the trail around a cabin-sized block of cracked volcanic rock, and stopped.

Ahead of him stood a saddled horse. A grulla. It was tied to a willow at the edge of the arroyo. The horse turned to look at Chaney. It twitched its ears and switched its tail and whickered softly. It stomped one of its rear hooves. That hoof and the other three hooves were wrapped in deer hide.

Chaney's heart leaped into his throat.

Movement above and to his right.

He whipped his head in that direction to see a tall, mustached man in a dark frock coat and black hat standing beside a boulder about thirty yards up the slope, on the northeast side of the canyon. The tall man shook his head gravely, jade eyes flashing in the afternoon sunlight, and pressed his cheek to the rear stock of the Henry rifle he was aiming into the canyon.

Flames lashed out of the Henry's octagonal barrel.

When Chaney heard the rifle's coughing report that whipped around the canyon like a thunderclap, he was already on the ground. He felt like someone had slammed a sledgehammer against his upper-left chest.

The rogue lawman lowered the rifle slightly and ejected the spent cartridge, which careened over his right shoulder to clatter off a rock behind him. He pumped a fresh round into the chamber and stared through his own powder smoke wafting in the air before him at the man lying supine in the canyon, grinding his spurs into the gravelly ground as he arched his back, death spasming through him.

He'd lost his hat. The high-crowned Stetson with a Texas crease lay several feet away to his left. He lifted his bald head and round face toward Hawk, his deputy US marshal's badge flashing in the sunlight from where it was pinned to his black bullhide vest over a white, blue-pinstriped shirt. He gritted his teeth beneath his gray-brown mustache.

Hawk cursed.

The man had jerked just as Hawk had fired, fouling the rogue lawman's aim. He'd meant to kill the man outright. He felt he owed him that much — for working a damned hard job for low pay, if for no other reason.

Hawk aimed again. His second shot blew the top of the man's head off and lay him flat down on the ground, boots shaking with the last of his death spasms.

Beyond him, on the other side of the large, black boulder, men shouted. A horse whinnied.

Hooves clacked on rock.

Hawk racked a fresh round into his Henry's breech. A second later, the clattering died. A horse whickered down the canyon a few yards. Hawk crouched low, holding his Henry up high across his chest, waiting.

Silence.

A hot, dry breeze blew against his back. It lifted dust along the canyon floor beneath him, and swirled it. When the mini-cyclone died, a hatted head and the end of a rifle barrel slid out from the left side of the large, black boulder.

Hawk slapped the Henry's butt plate to his shoulder, aimed quickly, and fired.

The hatted head jerked back violently. The man's entire body was revealed to Hawk as he staggered away from the boulder, to its left side, throwing his arms out and dropping his rifle. He stumbled over a rock behind him, and fell hard. Arms and legs akimbo, he jerked as his life left him.

Hawk pursed his lips with satisfaction. That man had likely not even heard the shot that had blown his lamp out.

Pumping a fresh round, Hawk dropped to a knee beside his covering rock, looking around, waiting. The third lawman was out here somewhere. He'd glassed all three on his back trail. If the lawman was smart, knowing that his two partners were dead, he'd mount up and ride off.

But if he'd been smart, he wouldn't have headed after Hawk in the first place.

Hawk held his position for ten minutes, growing impatient. He didn't want to have to kill any more lawmen. He wanted to be after Pima Miller. But he could do nothing until he'd scoured the third lawman off his trail.

Something moved along the slope on the canyon's west side. Hawk drew back behind his boulder as a slug slammed into the opposite side of it, spanging wickedly. At the same time, the belching report reached Hawk's ears. It screeched around the canyon for several seconds.

Then the man fired again. And again.

After the last echo had died, Hawk doffed his hat and edged a look around his boulder. His keen eyes picked out the silhouetted hat and rifle barrel halfway up the canyon's west slope. Smoke was wafting in the air around the silhouette.

Hawk snaked his Henry around the side of his covering boulder and snapped off two quick shots, driving the shooter back behind a rock. Then Hawk donned his hat, bolted out from behind the boulder, and dashed around boulders and cacti, heading toward the opposite side of the canyon.

He wove through his cover like a stalking cat. The third lawman, Alvin Something-or-other, flung lead at him from the canyon's west slope. The shots screeched off rocks and plunked into saguaros and barrel cactus, raking several stems from a clump of Mormon tea. As Hawk jogged steadily along the canyon's north slope, which was the wall creating a box canyon, drawing nearer his quarry, Alvin grew more and more desperate.

His shots came faster and faster. They also came wilder and wilder.

Then there was a lull during which the man was probably reloading.

Hawk turned along the crease forming the canyon's northwest corner and began angling back downcanyon but also climbing the western slope at a slant, toward where he'd last seen Alvin's gun smoke waft. He heard the rifle crash again but could not see it from his current vantage. As he rounded a boulder and a one-armed saguaro, he saw the muzzle flash and the smoke puff.

The slug curled the air off Hawk's left shoulder.

Hawk dropped to one knee and raised his Henry. He fired just as the third lawman snapped his eyes wide in fear and pulled his head back behind a nub of rock protruding from a bed of black shale about forty yards farther up the slope.

Hawk's slug hammered the side of the rock nub, keeping the third lawman back behind his cover. Hawk lowered the Henry, and, levering another round into the sixteen-shooter's chamber, ran up the slope, zigzagging between saguaros and boulders and piles of porous volcanic rock blown out of the earth's bowels eons ago.

The shooter fired two more rounds at him. Both flew wide. Hawk kept scrambling up the slope toward the shooter's cover. He wended his way through rocks and prickly pear, ran up past Alvin's boulder and threw himself to the ground, aiming his Henry at the backside of the rock from where Alvin Something-or-other had been shooting.

Alvin wasn't there.

Hawk saw him scrambling up the slope toward the ridge crest. He had his rifle in one hand. His boots were slipping on shale, and he was pushing off the ground with his other hand.

Hawk heaved himself to his feet, sent two quick rounds after the third lawman, and then ran up the slope behind him. Alvin glanced over his right shoulder at Hawk. His eyes widened. He was grunting and cursing under his breath, breathing hard.

He threw himself behind a rock little larger than a gravestone. Hawk saw the end of the man's rifle barrel snake around the side of the rock.

Hawk dropped to his belly and raised the Henry. A ratcheting hiss rose from ten feet in front of him, on the upslope. The diamondback was tightly coiled, button tail raised. It was sliding its flat head toward Hawk, forked tongue extended, its little, colorless eyes like tarnished pellets.

Just as the serpent appeared about to strike, Hawk blew its head off. Its headless body struck, anyway. The bloody, ragged end where its head had been fell into the dirt and gravel about a foot in front of Hawk, writhing.

The rogue lawman pumped a fresh cartridge and took aim again at the shooter's rock.

"Hold on!" the man screamed.

He'd come out from behind the rock, moving backward up the slope. He tossed his rifle away and continued stumbling backward.

"Don't shoot me!" Alvin screamed.

He'd lost his hat and his curly blond hair was caked with dust and bits of foliage. Sweat ran down his narrow cheeks. Hawk lowered the Henry, aiming it out from his hip, and strode up the slope. By the time Hawk reached the third lawman, Alvin had reached the flat, gravelly top of the ridge, a barrel cactus rising on his right.

Buzzards were circling high but quartering over the canyon in which the two dead lawmen lay.

Alvin stopped, thrust his hands up, palms out.

"Please don't shoot me. Ah, Jesus!"

Hawk stopped six feet in front of the young lawman. "You damn fool."

"Please . . . don't!" Alvin turned his head away as though he couldn't bear to look at the man who was about to kill him.

"Why'd you do it, you damn fool? Why did you get your two partners killed?"

"Ah, shit," Alvin said, licking his dry, dusty lips. "There's a reward. A big one. Governors of four territories got together, set a bounty. Twenty thousand dollars to any lawman who can prove they killed you!"

Hawk had heard about the reward, though he hadn't been sure it wasn't a mere rumor. There were lots of rumors — lies — regarding his exploits. A few years ago several territorial governors had put out a death warrant on him.

Now, this.

Hawk chuckled without mirth. "Twenty thousand dollars ain't worth a pinch of rock salt if you ain't alive to spend it."

"I know that," Alvin said. "I know that now."

"You got your partners killed."

"I know that!"

There was a dribbling sound. Hawk looked down to see that the inside of Alvin's left pants leg was wet. Liquid has splashed atop his boot, slithered down the side of the sole to roll up in the dirt.

"Drop that pistol belt," Hawk ordered.

Alvin unbuckled and dropped his pistol and shell belt inside of five seconds.

"Forget about your horse. You start walkin' north and don't stop or take even one look back, hear?"

Alvin stared at Hawk, lips trembling. "Hell, I'll die out here without my horse, my gun!"

"You'll make it back to the Superstition

station. You'll be hurtin', but you'll make it. Unless you want me to shoot you right here, which, when I think about it, is all you deserve."

"No! No . . . I'll make it, all right."

"If I ever see you again, Alvin, I ain't gonna be near as generous."

"No."

"Move!" Hawk bellowed, stepping around behind the frightened lawman.

Alvin glanced back at him and then, keeping his hands raised to his shoulders, began running down the slope at an angle, heading for the canyon bottom.

Behind him, Hawk shouted, "Drag that soggy boot back north and live to piss another day, *friend*!"

CHAPTER 11
THE OUTLAW'S DILEMMA

As her Morgan lurched up an incline through greasewood and barrel cactus, Jodi glanced over her shoulder, and smiled.

Miller scowled. "What the hell you grinnin' at? You simple?"

The girl did not reply but turned her horse into a crease between two large chunks of sandstone rising from the top of the hill they were on. Miller gave a wry chuff and followed her through the crease. On the other side, the girl slid lithely down from her Morgan's back and stood looking around, her gloved fists on her hips.

"What the hell you doin'?" Miller raked out at her. "It's too early to stop."

"Not if we're where we're goin'."

"Huh?"

"This is the place I said you get could set up your bushwhack, kill that rogue lawman fella." She grinned at him again.

Miller looked around. More mushrooms

of sandstone rose before him. Mesquites and cedars grew up out of cracks in the rock. Sandstone boulders stood among the growth. Miller swung down from the back of his brindle bay, tied the horse to a cedar, and then climbed up the shelving mush-rooms of sandstone rock.

At the crest, he could see out over a deep, narrow valley. Really, it was more of a gorge. There were a couple of lower ridges between Miller's position and the larger canyon on the far side of which jutted an even steeper ridge than the one he was on. From here, the main canyon looked like a mere crease between ridges. He could see it where it doglegged off to his right and away.

"Best get away from the ridge, silly," Jodi said, slapping his upper arm with the back of her hand.

"Why?"

She pointed at the doglegging canyon to Miller's right. "Because if he's still on our trail, he's down there somewhere. Might see us."

Miller pointed. "That's where we came from?"

Jodi nodded. "We rode right up here — or nearly so, anyway — about an hour ago. Then circled back. The canyon trail passes about sixty yards below where we're standing." She nodded toward the canyon side of the ridge. "He'll follow our trail and you can dry gulch him from here."

Miller stared down the far side of the ridge, saw the trail angling from his right to his left beyond some rocks, catclaw, and cedar shrubs. "Shit, we rode past here. Crazy damn country."

The girl chuckled, self-satisfied.

"So he'll ride right past here — *down there.*" Miller laughed and ran a gloved hand across his chin. "Yeah, that'll work."

Getting a handle on the layout, he stepped back a little, until a large thumb of sandstone and granite partly shielded him from view from the broader canyon below. "Shit — this is some crazy country. Talk about a devil's playground!"

"A fella could get lost without a good guide, couldn't he?" Jodi's tone was customarily jibing.

Miller snorted at her. But she was right. He didn't like it, but he needed her. There was such a maze of canyons in this neck of the Superstitions that a man could walk thirty yards, blink, turn around and be forever lost.

Miller retrieved his spyglass from his saddlebags, doffed his hat, and stood just off the corner of the large boulder capping the ridge. He trained the glass to the north-west, the direction from which the girl had led him, the direction from which his stalker would be coming, as well.

Miller stared for about fifteen minutes through the glass until he finally caught sight of a slow-moving shadow coming along the main canyon. A man was what the shadow appeared — a gray-brown man-shadow moving at a steady pace along Miller's back trail. The outlaw knew it was Hawk. Of course, it could be a prospector or some lone Indian, but Miller knew it was Hawk. He'd spied the same shadow on his trail early the day before, and he'd noticed it several times since.

Always moving at the same, maddeningly slow, plodding, steady speed. In no hurry whatever. Apparently, he was so sure of eventually running down his quarry that he felt no *need* to hurry.

Studying that slow-moving but purposeful shadow now moving toward him at a seeming snail's pace, Miller felt the short hairs along the back of his neck rise. His heart quickened. He remembered the man he'd seen in the yard of Nan-tee's shack, so coolly and sure-handedly dispatching Miller's second gang.

Some of the best shooters in the territory.

Maybe in all of the Southwest. He'd blown them all to hell and he would have blown Miller to hell, too, if Miller hadn't had the advantage of being in the cabin, where the shadows had concealed him.

One of Hawk's bullets had drilled Miller's woman. Too bad. But better her than him. Since that afternoon, the outlaw had only considered the child he'd left behind in passing and certainly with no degree of sentimentality. He hadn't even paused to consider who would care for the boy, whom Nan-tee had called Ti-Kwah, which in her language meant sunrise.

Or was it sun*set*?

He lowered the spyglass, donned his hat, and stepped back behind the boulder.

The girl was sitting on a rock, her back to a cedar growing up through a jagged crack running through the sandstone. She'd removed her hat and was wiping moisture from the sweatband with a spruce-green handkerchief.

"This is a special place for me," she told Miller, smiling fondly as she looked around. The large dimpled areas in the sandstone held water from last night's monsoon rain.

"How so?"

She hiked a shoulder. Her smile grew broader. "I became a woman here. On a blanket right down there."

As usual concerning this girl, Miller was incredulous. "What's that?"

"I told you — I became a *woman* here." Jodi dropped to her knees and drank from one of the rainwater-filled dimples.

"You became a woman here," Miller said, skeptically.

Jodi lifted her head, sat back on her heels, donned her hat, and looked around. "One of Geronimo's warriors found me here. Took me by surprise. Didn't seem to know whether to kill me or take me, so he *took* me. And then I killed him. Stuck one of his own arrows through his neck."

Miller just stared at her. She'd said it as though she'd just recounted a mildly successful fishing trip.

She turned her head toward him, smiled, and blinked slowly. Her eyes were dull with threat.

"Why, you're crazy," Miller said, sliding his right hand to the holster thonged on his right thigh. It brushed only leather. He looked down at it, lower jaw hanging. When he looked at the girl, she reached around behind her. When she brought her right hand forward, she was holding his Remington.

"Lookin' for this?" she asked, closing her

upper teeth over her lower lip.

"How in the *hell* . . . ?"

As she held the gun, she raised and lowered the hammer a little with her thumb, making a faint clicking sound. "You oughta know by now, Mister Outlaw, that I ain't no little girl you should trifle with."

"How did you get my gun?" Miller demanded, facing her, spreading his boots a little more than shoulder width apart.

"Wouldn't you like to know?"

"I'll take that back."

"Why? So you can shoot me with it?"

Miller raised his voice. He didn't want to admit it, but his mouth was dry with fear. "I said I'll take that back, you little . . . !"

He let his voice trail off. She was staring at him, one eye sort of slanted in toward her nose. It was more than just a faintly devilish look. That look coupled with his pistol resting in the palm of her right hand rocked him back on his heels.

"Oh, here!" she said, tossing it up to him.

He stumbled back, catching the gun against his chest. His face was warm with embarrassment. Anger and rage made his knees feel as though they were filled with warm mud.

"Did you believe all that?"

Miller lowered the gun. "All what?"

"My story about the brave I killed?"

"Should I?"

Kneeling there on the stone-capped crest of the ridge, she smiled at him again while staring up at him from beneath her blonde brows and the low-canted brim of her hat. "If I was you, I would. And I'd also keep in mind, I got a knife in my boot. And I got this here."

She reached around behind her again. When she showed him her right hand, it was again filled with a pistol. A .41-caliber pocket pistol with ivory grips.

"Stole this off a gambler passin' through the station," Jodi said, hefting the wicked-looking little popper in her hand. "Figured it might come in handy someday."

She tossed it from hand to hand before tucking it back behind her, and rising. "Well, I reckon we'd best tend the horses and set up camp," she said with a sigh, turning away and skipping down the rocks. The little pistol was tucked behind her wide, brown belt, at the small of her slender back. "Probably gonna rain again like it usually does."

Watching her, Miller canted his head to one side and raked the fingers of his left hand down through the ginger whiskers on his cheek.

Later, after a brief rain, Miller took Old Man Zimmerman's Winchester and had a look around his and Jodi's camp.

They were on the side of a larger mountain from the top of which, staring southwest, Miller could see the formation known as Weaver's Needle. Most folks in the territory had heard about the "Dutchman," some fellow named Walzer, who'd discovered an old Mexican gold mine somewhere near Weaver's Needle, which some folks called "Sombrero" because it was also shaped like the steepled crown of the Mexican hat.

Like many who'd spent more than a week in Arizona Territory and had heard about the vein that was so rich you could literally use a hammer to break the nearly pure ore out of the walls and fill enough of a poke in just a few minutes to put yourself on easy street for the rest of your life, Miller had had a hankering to look for the mine himself.

But there were other stories, too.

Stories about many men who'd tried looking for the same mine, but the country was such a maze of cactus and rattlesnake-infested ravines and canyons that they'd become forever lost, died of thirst or starvation, been tortured and killed by Apaches, or had stumbled out of the Superstitions avoiding such fates by a hair's breadth and had vowed never to return, warning others not to try it.

Miller had heeded such warnings. Not necessarily because he feared anything the Superstitions could throw at him, but because he was basically a lazy man and preferred to make his living by a much easier means.

By stealing it from others.

Still, that brown finger of crenellated rock jutting above the cactus-studded hogbacks held an eerie fascination even for a lazy man like Pima Miller. Imagine walking into an ancient gold mine, the walls around you sparkling with gold so rich and pure it hardly needed smelting!

Miller brushed a fist across his chin, shook his head, and made his way back down the craggy peak he was on. As he did so, he stopped near a sandstone shelf, and stared down, frowning. A hoofprint marked the sandstone gravel and red caliche to the right of his right boot.

A hoofprint. Looking around, he saw several more. Two riders had passed along this mountainside, following what appeared a game trail or maybe an ancient Indian trail. The Superstitions, having been claimed for centuries by the Chiricahua Apaches, were woven with such traces. And the mount of neither rider had been shod.

Unshod horses meant Indian.

Around here, *Apache* Indian.

Chiricahua.

Miller could tell that the Chiricahuas had passed here maybe an hour before the brief rain of an hour earlier.

Cold fingers of apprehension raking his spine — Miller had heard plenty of stories of Apache torture — he dropped to a knee and studied the terrain around him. Spying no movement outside of a jackrabbit and a cactus wren perched atop a nearby saguaro, he continued on down the mountain.

He kept a .44 round seated in his carbine's chamber, his thumb on the off-cocked hammer.

By the time he saw the brindle bay and the Morgan tied to ironwood shrubs below his and the girl's camp, where they could drink from natural tanks filled with fresh rainwater, the sky had again turned the color of oily rags. Thunder rumbled like a giant's upset stomach.

Cold raindrops began splattering against the back of Miller's neck, making him wince against the chill in sharp contrast to the earlier, searing heat.

He walked up the grade beyond the horses and into the rocks where he and the girl had set up camp on a level, cactus-free strip of ground at the base of the ridge crest from where he intended to rid his trail of Hawk. The clearing was surrounded by tall boulders and cedars, which offered some protection from the rain. Jodi had erected a burlap lean-to angling out from one of the shrubs. She lay under it now, resting her head against her saddle, hat tipped down over her eyes. Her arms were folded atop her chest, boots crossed at the ankles.

Jodi appeared to be asleep, gold-blonde hair falling messily across the saddle.

Watching her, Miller's loins tingled. At the same time, apprehension continued to play a needling rhythm tapped out with cold fingers against his backbone. The girl was damned dangerous. He'd have to kill her sooner or later.

Now might be a good time, before she could get the drop on him. True, he needed her to lead him out of the mountains, but something told him she wouldn't let him get that far. Not far enough to feel independent of her.

Because she knew he'd kill her then.

He wasn't sure what her game was, but she was up to something. Could be he was just being nervy, but he didn't think so. Possibly, she knew about the twelve hundred-dollar bounty on his head, though it might have gone up since Kingman. And all the torture — even Apache torture — wouldn't drag the secret out of the girl before she was ready to fess up. Miller had a keen, stone-cold feeling at the base of his breastbone that if he waited to find out what her game was, and how high the stakes were, he would be too late to save himself.

He held his carbine across his belly. He squeezed the gun in his hands. As cold as it had suddenly turned, with the rain lashing him from behind, his hands were sweating inside his gloves.

A bass voice whispered in his ear. "Kill her, fool. The rogue lawman is as good as dead. Tomorrow, after you kill him, you'll have two spare horses, plenty of guns, ammo, and grub. You know where Weaver's Needle is. Once you get there, swing west and you'll be to Phoenix in no time. Rest up there with a whore or two, a couple bottles of whiskey, a game of cards, and head on down to the border."

Miller's heart hiccupped, increased its pace. His breath grew shallow. Sweat ran down the palms of his hands, inside his gloves. He squeezed the rifle again, pressing the sweat into his gloves. He slowly thumbed the hammer back. The thunder and the rain covered the clicking sounds.

"Kill her now . . . before she kills you . . ."

Miller moved heavily forward, stopped just outside the lean-to, and stared down at the girl. His heart beat more persistently. He prodded her with his boot toe.

She used a gloved index finger to poke the brim of her hat up off her forehead. She turned to him, wrinkling the skin above the bridge of her nose. She continued to stare at him like that for a good half a minute. And then, so slowly so as to be almost imperceptible, her mouth corners rose.

Miller eased the Winchester's hammer back down.

His hands shaking, he leaned the rifle against the cedar's twisted trunk, doffed his hat, and crawled under the tarpaulin.

He woke the next morning to the smell of wood smoke. He rolled over and saw small flames licking up from several catclaw sticks. Jodi had a blanket thrown over her shoulders. It was all she was wearing. It didn't cover much of her.

She was just then filling a canteen from one of the natural rock tanks near the fire.

Miller cursed, grabbed a cedar log, and rubbed out the flames with a single swipe.

"You *crazy?*" the outlaw rasped, eyes nearly bulging from their sockets. "You tryin' to draw him in here, or *what?*"

CHAPTER 12
TURNABOUT

In the following dawn's misty shadows, Hawk followed the trail up a steep incline and into scattered cedars speckling this slope high above the main canyon. He swept his gaze from left to right and back again, and then, by instinct, he drew back on the grulla's reins.

He'd been extra cautious while following Pima Miller, because it had become obvious just after he'd killed the two federal lawmen and sent the third one hoofing it back north with a wet boot, that the girl was much more than a hostage.

She was, as Hawk had suspected, a guide.

She was also Miller's lover. He could tell that from the sign left at their bivouacs.

Hawk had learned much by studying her and Miller's tracks. He knew which horse was carrying which member of his two-party quarry from having seen two separate sets of boot prints near the separate horse prints, informing him which rider had mounted and dismounted which horse.

He knew that Miller's horse had a faint flaw in its right-rear hoof, and that the outlaw's horse was ever-so-slightly pigeon-toed. Not enough that the trait could likely be noticed by simply watching the horse walk or trot, but the indentions its shod feet left in the ground told the tale.

The girl's horse was almost always in the lead, while Miller rode behind her. She was guiding him into the mountains. That was the reason for Hawk's added caution.

He had little doubt that Miller would try to ambush him and that he'd instructed the girl to lead him to an opportune place from which to bring about the ambush. Thus, Hawk, who had set up his own ambushes and been the target of others' ambushes enough times to know what kind of terrain to look for, rode a little more slowly and with his eyes and ears especially skinned for trouble.

He sensed trouble now.

The secondary ridge on his left sloped gradually up toward a large, rectangular boulder set atop a broad sandstone dike screened in cedars and several different kinds of cactus, including a saguaro with one arm pointing down. The ridge was about seventy yards from the trail Hawk was following — the same trail that Miller and Jodi Zimmerman had followed sometime during the previous afternoon, before the rain.

A perfect distance and reasonable incline for accurate shooting by a seasoned shooter.

What also had alarms bells tolling in the rogue lawman's ears was the fact that Miller and the girl had ridden through here especially slowly, as though they'd known exactly where they were heading and were confident that, despite the storm clouds that had been building, they would arrive at their destination soon.

Hawk pulled back on the grulla's bridle reins. The horse gave a soft whicker, sensing its rider's caution, and backed up. Out of sight from the ridge, Hawk turned the grulla, rode a hundred yards back down the trail, and then turned the horse up the steep southern slope, climbing the ridge.

The grulla was sure-footed, mountain bred, and it had little trouble negotiating the incline's uncertain terrain stippled with the dangerous cholla, or "jumping" cactus, and several nasty-looking clumps of catclaw. When Hawk had gained the secondary ridge about seventy yards from where he assumed Miller was lying in ambush, he continued up the next ridge, and stopped the grulla several yards down the other side, among boulders whose pocks and pits offered the tired mount fresh rainwater.

He slipped the grulla's bit, loosened its latigo, and shucked his rifle from the saddle scabbard. He sat down on a rock to exchange his stockmen's boots for a pair of soft moccasins for easier, stealthier walking, and then headed back up and over the ridge.

Hawk moved slowly, stopping every four steps to drop to a knee to look all around him and to listen. Then he continued moving down the slope at a slant, in the direction of where he was assuming his quarry had holed up to set up an ambush.

He'd gained the lower ridge as the sun poked its head above the eastern horizon, spreading a saffron light across the stark, brown ridgetop behind him. Now he moved slower. Much slower, setting each moccasin down so slowly that neither foot made a sound.

The sun was full up, and Hawk could feel the heat building, when he finally brought up the backsides of a couple of horses tied to the base of the dike he'd spied from its other side. There was a gap in the rocks near the horses. He figured that would lead directly to Miller's and the girl's position.

But, because of the horses, it was no good.

He moved to his left, and it took him nearly a whole hour more to find access to the dike from the side opposite the horses. Slowly, he moved through several black boulders capping the dike, weaving among cedars and cacti. Suddenly, he stopped and dropped to a knee behind one of these boulders.

His heart thudded.

He smelled smoke on the breeze. Wood smoke.

For an instant, the smell confused him. Was Miller stupid enough to build a coffee fire when he knew that Hawk was moving toward him?

Hawk's hesitation distracted him. He was just about to turn and retreat when a shadow angled down on the rock slab near his right shoulder and knee. The click of a gun hammer sounded as loud as a war drum in his left ear.

The cold, round barrel was rammed up taut against the back of his head, just behind that ear.

"Don't so much as twitch, Hawk," said the menacingly reasonable voice of Pima Miller. "Just lower that Henry's hammer and set it down slow. One quick move and I'll drill a forty-four round through your brain. Don't want to, 'cause this close I'm liable to get covered in your oozin's. But I will." He heard the man's smile in what came next. "You know I will."

Hawk's heart thudded heavily. A keen frustration coupled with humiliation was a hard rock in his belly.

He'd been outsmarted. They'd figured — maybe *planned* — on him finding their camp. They'd built the fire to confuse him. It had worked. He'd let his quarry get behind him. An unforgiveable mistake. One he would deservedly pay for.

Breaking through the stiff mortar of his sharp reluctance, he lowered the Henry's hammer and set the gun down on the rock slab before him.

"Now, both pistols. Set 'em down there next to the rifle. *Slow.*"

Hawk rolled his eyes to the right. Miller had backed up a few feet, holding his cocked pistol about four feet away from Hawk's head. Too far to lunge at him with any hope of being successful.

Hawk drew a deep breath. He slid the Russian and the Colt from their holsters. The snick of steel against leather was a sickening sound.

"Easy, now," Miller said behind him, shifting his weight from one boot to the other.

The nervousness in the man's voice only slightly tempered Hawk's chagrin at having given them the drop.

Hawk set the pistols down by the rifle.

"Get them hands up, *stand* up, and turn around slow."

Hawk raised his hands to his shoulders and turned around. Miller was about three inches shorter than the rogue lawman. The outlaw backed up a step, swabbed his lips with his tongue, twitched a smile. "Feelin' foolish?" He chuckled, continuing to shift his weight around on his hips and opening and closing his hand around the neck of his Remington's butt. "I bet you are. I bet you're feelin' right foolish!"

Footsteps sounded behind Miller. And then the girl appeared, making her way down a pile of hard, black lava flanking Miller on his left. Tawny hair tumbled to her shoulders as she let the rise's momentum carry her down the lava pile.

As she stopped at the bottom, flushed and a little breathless, she smiled, showing white teeth between pink lips. She drew her shoulders back, pushing her breasts out.

She said, "Holy shit — you got him."

She'd said it quietly, awe in her tone.

"Yep," Miller said. "I got him."

"So, that's him — the rogue lawman." The

girl was walking toward Hawk, sort of swinging her hips and thrusting her breasts.

She stopped beside Miller. Her hazel eyes sparkled as she gazed up at the dark, grim-faced man before her. "Big, tall drink of water, ain't he?" she said, raking her eyes up and down his frame and across his broad shoulders, hooking her thumbs in her back trouser pockets.

Miller lunged forward. Aiming the pistol in his right hand at Hawk's face, he buried his left fist in Hawk's gut.

The sudden move had caught the rogue lawman off guard. Miller was a strong son of a bitch — Hawk would give him that. The savage blow rammed Hawk's solar plexus back against his spine, compressing his lungs and forcing his wind out in a single, coughing chuff. Hawk's knees buckled. He hit the stone-hard ground, leaning forward, arms crossed on his belly, gasping.

Miller stepped back quickly, slanting his cocked pistol down at Hawk's head. "There — that sorta shortens him up a little, don't it?"

Rage swept through Hawk as he tried to suck air back into his lungs. His upper lip quivered as he curled it above his mouth and glared up at the grinning, narrow-eyed, ginger-bearded killer standing over him.

151

"Ha-ha!" Miller laughed, taking another nervous step back, as though away from a leg-trapped bear. "He didn't like that."

The girl seemed to be enjoying herself. She smiled down at Hawk, her eyes bright and shifting between the two men. She resembled a bloodthirsty spectator at a bare-knuckle bout. But then, suddenly, her smile became a frown as she turned to Miller. "Well, ain't you gonna kill him?"

"Not unless he tries somethin'. This man has a bounty on his head — the most I ever saw."

"Huh?"

"Sure enough," Miller said. "Uncle Sam has put a twenty-thousand-dollar bounty on his head. All I gotta do is turn him into the nearest federal marshal to make my claim."

"Forget it," the girl said, shaking her head. "Forget it, Pima. We can do better than that."

Miller looked at her, narrowing his eyes impatiently. "You just get back to the fire and put a pot of coffee on. Me, I'm thirsty an' hungry. I done just captured the rogue lawman his ownself!"

"Forget it, Pima. You'd best shoot this son of a bitch, or you'll regret it."

Miller gave her a mocking grin. "Now, now — no need to be scared, little angel girl. I can tame this wildcat. Come on, Hawk. Get to your feet, turn around and keep goin' the way you was goin' before you was so rudely interrupted."

Miller chuckled again at that, but Hawk could still hear the nervous, almost giddy edge in the killer's voice.

Hawk had regained his wind though his lungs still felt pinched. He looked up at the gun Miller kept aimed at his head. Then he looked past the Remington's cocked hammer at Miller's face. The man was sweating and grinning, and Hawk wanted nothing more than to hammer the killer's face with his fists.

In good time.

Slowly, he gained his feet, wincing at the spike-like pain in his belly, the pinched feeling in his lungs. He donned his hat, letting the rawhide chin thong dangle to his chest, and then turned, stepped over his weapons, and began moving through the rocks in the direction of the fire. The fire's smoke thickened as he approached.

He stared down from the escarpment at a burlap-roofed lean-to in a small hollow among rocks. The fire lay on the other side of it. It had been built with cedar mixed with cottonwood branches to which green leaves still clung, making smoke.

"Gotta hand it to her," Miller said a ways behind him, keeping his distance. "That was the girl's idea."

"Jodi's idea," the girl said. "I got a name, Pima. Feel free to use it."

Miller chuckled at that, as well. "Fooled you — didn't it, Hawk? For a second there you thought I was dumb enough to build a fire, knowin' you was on my trail. You thought you was just gonna waltz right in and surprise us."

"Yep, you fooled me," Hawk admitted. For a second it had been true. At least, they'd baffled him long enough to move up on him. He deserved the jeering. But he hoped he'd get another chance at Miller. Doubtful, but hope kept a man alive when it was all he had.

The hope of a kill. Two kills, now, since the girl had thrown in with Miller.

Fueling that hope was the fact that Hawk had a pearl-gripped, over-and-under derringer in an inside pocket of his frock coat. As well as a short-but-deadly, antler-gripped dagger in his right boot.

Miller pressed the Remy's barrel against the small of Hawk's back. Instantly, without having to consider the move, he swung around, pinwheeling his left arm. But Miller had been anticipating the ploy, and the

154

killer managed to pull his hand and pistol back and out of Hawk's reach, so that Hawk's fingers only brushed the end of the Remy's barrel.

Hawk froze. Miller laughed his insufferable laugh.

Flanking him, the girl shook her head slowly, darkly. "Pima, you'd best quit funnin' and kill this man before he kills you. Before he kills us both."

That riled the killer once more. Scowling at her, he said, "I thought I told you to make coffee?"

"Kill him, Pima!"

"I'm the ramrod of this little two-man gang, sweet darlin'!" Miller railed, disciplined enough to keep his eyes on Hawk. "So kindly shut your pretty mouth. It's a might better at different things than yappin', if'n you get my drift. You get over there to the fire and make me a *goddamn pot of coffee*!"

He was looking at the girl now. But Hawk did not move on him. Miller was cagey. Hawk had to bide his time. Hoping, of course, that the girl didn't get her way and he still *had* some time.

Glancing darkly at Hawk, her jaws hard, Jodi Zimmerman swung wide of both men and made her way down to the fire.

"Now, you head on down there, too, Mister Rogue Lawman, sir," Miller ordered. "But first . . ." He grinned broadly, narrowing his little, narrow eyes. "I'd like you to remove that little popper you got residin' inside your coat."

Hawk stared at the man grinning back at him.

Slowly, he removed the derringer from his coat pocket, and tossed it to Miller. Miller pocketed the derringer, jerked his chin toward the lean-to. Hawk turned around and made his way into the diamondback's den of Miller's camp.

Well, he still had the dagger.

At least, for now.

CHAPTER 13
IN THE DIAMONDBACK'S DEN

Keeping his Remington aimed at Hawk, Miller reached into a cavy sack and pulled out a coiled rope. He tossed the rope onto the ground beside the girl, who'd just filled a coffeepot from a canteen.

"Tie him," Miller ordered.

She glared up at him. "You wanted me to make coffee!"

"Tie him first. Tie his wrists together, behind his back. Then tie his ankles. You, Mister Rogue Lawman — you sit down in front of that rock over there."

Hawk looked at the rock. It was on the far side of the little hollow from the lean-to and the fire.

Jodi looked at Miller. "You wouldn't have to worry about him if you'd shoot him."

Miller closed his eyes for a second. When he'd slowly opened them, his face was red. He drew a deep breath as though to calm himself. "If you backtalk me one more

157

time . . ."

"Oh, all right!" the girl said, angrily tossing the coffeepot against a nearby boulder and grabbing the rope.

She walked over to where Hawk had sat down against the rock. Miller holstered his pistol, picked up a carbine, cocked it, and aimed it out from his right thigh at Hawk's head, to one side of the girl.

"One wrong move, Mister Rogue Lawman, I'll drill ya another eye."

Hawk just stared up at him.

"Lean forward and get those arms behind your back," the girl ordered from six feet away.

Hawk stared up at her, his green eyes without expression, and then he slowly complied. He gave the girl a faintly challenging look, quirking his mouth corners.

She glanced uncertainly at Miller. "You gonna shoot him if he jumps me?"

"I'll shoot him."

"You hear that, mister?" the girl said, fear coloring her cheeks and beetling her sun-bleached eyebrows. "He'll shoot you if you try anything."

Hawk said nothing. He just stared up at her with subtle menace.

The girl snorted, her jaws hard, and then she slid her eyes toward Miller once more before leaning forward, as though she were approaching the cage of a wild, freshly captured beast. Which, to her, Hawk guessed he was.

She dropped to a knee beside him and, flicking her gaze between his hands and his eyes, she wrapped the ropes around his wrists. As she stared at him, the expression in her eyes changed from apprehension to a faintly pensive cunning. He held her gaze for a time, and he got the sense that Miller had taken on a real load when he'd taken the girl away from the Superstition Station.

"What the hell you smilin' at?" Miller said.

"He ain't smiling," Jodi said, grunting as she tied a knot in the rope binding Hawk's wrists. "He's smirkin'. He knows that every second that goes by that you don't kill him, he still has a chance of killin' both of us." She stared into Hawk's gaze. "Ain't that right, mister?"

Hawk didn't say anything. The rope was cutting into his wrists.

The girl smiled, signaling a definite change in her mood. She cut the rope with a barlow knife and used the other half to bind Hawk's ankles, keeping her gaze for the most part on his, as though probing him with her shrewd, cunning mind. She glanced at Miller and then back at Hawk, her forehead creased pensively.

And then she stood and stepped away from Hawk's bound feet.

"Now, then," Miller said. "You ain't so tough, now, are ya, Mister Rogue Lawman, sir?"

The outlaw grinned as he stepped toward Hawk. The killer lifted the barrel of his carbine, swung up its brass butt, and smashed it savagely against Hawk's left cheek.

Hawk grunted as the blow slammed his head sideways against the rock.

A high-pitched screech rose in his ears and flares exploded behind his squeezed-shut eyelids as he felt the angry welt swell on his cheek. Another welt, like a smoking brand, was rising on the back of his head. He felt the wetness of blood just beneath his right eye. It dribbled down his cheek toward his jawline.

Miller laughed.

Then he lunged toward Hawk again, ramming the carbine's butt against the left side of Hawk's mouth. Again, the back of Hawk's head hammered the rock behind him. His mouth burned. He tasted the copper of blood from the cut on the inside of his upper lip. His left eyetooth throbbed.

He felt blood dribble down from the

outside left corner of his mouth.

Rage boiled within him. He tried to draw back on it. Rage was a waste of energy as long as he was trussed up like a hog for the slaughter.

Still, he gritted his teeth, ignoring the barking of his left eyetooth, which felt loose, and glared up at Miller grinning down at him. Miller thrust the butt of his carbine toward Hawk once more, and the rogue lawman braced himself for another blow, squeezing his eyes closed.

"Now, ain't you tough!" the girl said sarcastically. "Beating up a tied man!"

Miller stopped the rifle about four inches from Hawk's face. He looked at the girl, pursing his lips and flaring his nostrils.

"First you wanna dry gulch him," she said. "Now you wanna beat him senseless when he can't fight back." She pulled her folding knife out of her jeans pocket, and opened it. "Let me untie him. Then you two can go at it, even odds."

She held Miller's gaze with a mocking one of her own.

And then she hardened her voice as she said, "Either that or kill him. But if you keep beatin' on a defenseless man, Pima, I'm gonna think you can't handle no other kind."

Miller whipped his head back toward Hawk. His close-set eyes seemed set even closer together. They were wide with pent-up fury. He aimed the carbine's barrel at Hawk's head, and clicked the hammer back.

Hawk stared at the rifle's small, round, black maw.

As black as death.

Here it comes, he thought.

He was mildly surprised that he felt no trepidation whatever. In fact, a strange calm washed over him. He felt his mouth corners spread an almost affable smile as he continued to gaze up at the man he thought was sure to kill him.

But in Hawk's mind, he was not seeing Pima Miller. He was seeing Linda and Jubal. They were standing on a green hill in the far distance, so he couldn't see them clearly, just their silhouettes, mainly, and the fact that Linda was wearing a frilly dress that was nearly the same rich yellow as her hair.

They were smiling, beckoning. A warm wind was blowing the skirt of Linda's yellow dress and her and Jubal's hair.

They were beckoning to him. His family was beckoning him home. Vaguely, as he stared toward them, wanting to get up from

162

the ground and run to them, he felt a tear ooze out the corner of his right eye and roll slowly down along his nose toward his mustache.

The bullet did not come.

The mirage faded, and Hawk found himself staring up at Pima Miller, incredulous. "What're you waiting for?"

The rifle sagged in Miller's arms. As the killer stared down at Hawk, his expression was faintly surprised, befuddled.

The girl owned much the same countenance. Her lips were slightly parted, hair hanging down along both sides of her face. Her breasts rose and fell behind her shirt as she breathed.

"Nah," Miller said. "Ain't much fun in killin' a man who ain't afraid to die." He depressed the carbine's hammer and lowered the barrel. "All in good time," he said. "All in good time."

He turned to Jodi. "Where's that coffee?"

The girl held her openly fascinated gaze on Hawk. Then she turned to Miller as though she'd forgotten he was there. She smiled and started walking toward the fire. Casting her amused smile at Hawk, she said, "Comin' right up!"

Hawk was disappointed.

He'd thought he was going home.

■ ■ ■ ■

The day passed slowly. For Hawk, sitting back against the boulder with his smashed face, it also passed miserably though the pain dulled after an hour or so.

What caused the bulk of the misery was knowing he'd been fooled. And having to watch Miller and Jodi stroll about the camp without being able to kill them.

The two had decided to stay put for the day, resting themselves as well as their horses. Miller's bullet wound still bothered the killer, which was plain from the stiff way he moved and by the long nap he took under the lean-to, while an afternoon thundershower soaked Hawk to the bone.

The girl joined the killer and when they woke up, they didn't seem to mind that Hawk was sitting only a few feet away. They coupled like back-alley curs, grunting and cursing and laughing throatily. Jodi seemed to like that Hawk could watch if he wanted to, and since he didn't have much choice, he saw her glance toward him now and then, while her hair jostled across her bare shoulders and jouncing breasts.

When they were done and dressed, the rain had stopped. The girl smiled once more at Hawk as she threw her hair back behind her shoulders and began looking for dry wood with which to build a fire.

Earlier, Miller had sent the girl off to retrieve Hawk's horse, and they'd picketed the grulla with their own. Hawk couldn't see the horses from his position, but he recognized his own mount's sporadic, nervous whickers. The grulla was no doubt able to smell Hawk, maybe even smell the dried blood on his rider's face, but he could not see him.

That fact and the strangers' presence made the horse owly.

It didn't do much for Hawk's mood, either.

As Miller and the girl sat around the fire that night, eating a jackrabbit the girl had snared and roasted, she said over her steaming coffee cup, canting her head toward Hawk, "How do you intend to turn him in for that reward money when you yourself got a bounty on your head?"

Miller forked meat and beans into his mouth and stared at her dully while he chewed. Then he picked something from between his teeth with his fingers, rubbed it on his trouser leg, and said with menacing nonchalance, "How do you know I got a bounty on my head?"

"I don't know," the girl said, hiking a shoulder. "Don't you?"

"You *know* I do."

"I *figured* you did," she said, hardening her voice with strained patience.

"That mean somethin' to you?"

Jodi studied him. She held her plate on one thigh, her coffee cup on the other thigh.

"Yeah," she said after several seconds, adding slowly, carefully enunciating every word as though for a moron to understand: "It means how in the hell do you think you're going to turn in that big drink of water over there for that twenty thousand dollars you say he's got on his head, when you yourself are wanted? I'd spell it out for you if I thought you could read!"

It was Miller's turn to study her with menacing blandness. After a while he said, quietly defensive, "I can read."

"What?"

"I can read, goddamnit!"

Jodi glanced over at Hawk, sitting about ten feet away. Hawk watched them, biding his time, waiting, since that was about all he could do, anyway. He sensed something happening between them. Something that might work in his favor, but he wasn't sure what that might be.

Meanwhile, he was quietly straining his

wrists behind his back, trying to work the girl's knot in the ropes free. It didn't look good. She'd tied a damned tight double knot, and so far, after several hours of spontaneous work on it, he hadn't made much, if any progress, but only caused his nails to bleed.

"What're you lookin' at him for?" Miller asked the girl.

"I was wonderin' if he was makin' any more sense out of you than I am."

"Don't look at him. He ain't there. You just keep your mooncalf eyes off him. He's my worry — not yours."

"Oh, that's right — it was the bounty on your head we was talking about. And how is it you figured to turn him in, when —"

"That's what you're here for."

Again, Jodi stared across the fire at Miller as though she were having trouble understanding him.

"You don't have a bounty on your head, do you?" Miller asked her.

"None that I know of."

"So . . ."

"So I'm gonna turn that man over to the first US marshal we run into."

"Just his head." Miller grinned and looked at Hawk. "Once when we get close to Tucson, were there's an old drunken deputy

US marshal posted, we'll shoot the son of a bitch, throw his head into a gunnysack, and *you'll* turn it over to old Hiram Mitchell and fill out the paperwork to put in for the reward. And when it comes, we'll split it."

"Fifty-fifty?"

"Sure," Miller said, hiking a shoulder. "I'm a fair man."

Jodi glanced over at Hawk once more. The firelight sparkled in her hazel eyes, blazed in certain strands of her hair flowing down over her shoulders.

She set her plate aside and used a scrap of burlap to remove the smoking coffeepot from the fire. She refilled both Miller's cup as well as her own and then returned the pot to the rock near the fire's glowing coals and short, dancing flames.

She sat back down, picked up her cup, and blew on it, the steam bathing her pretty face. "How do I know I can trust you?" she asked Miller.

"How do I know I can trust *you*?" Miller returned, leaning back against his saddle and crossing his legs at the ankles. "How do I know you ain't figurin' on turnin' me in for the reward on *my* head?"

"How much reward you got on your head?"

"Enough."

"How much?"

"Enough, I said."

The girl didn't let him off that easy. "How much?" she asked, gritting her own teeth and leaning toward him, hardening her jaws. She gave it as well as she got it, Hawk mused, still straining at the ropes binding his wrists.

Miller stared at her, blinked, glanced away, sheepish, and then returned his gaze to her. "Twelve hundred."

"Hah!" Jodi laughed, slapping her thigh. She hooked a thumb toward Hawk. "He's got twenty thousand on his head and you got twelve hundred on yours, and you think I'd take *yours* over *his*?"

Miller sat up, glaring at her and gritting his teeth again. "Just 'cause he has twenty thousand on his head and I only got twelve hundred don't mean a damn thing. It just means he's been at it longer, that's all! And, shit, he's a lawman! He makes them other lawmen look like fools!"

"Oh, take the hump out of your neck, Pima. I don't need your bounty, and I don't need his bounty, neither. And you don't need his bounty, neither. Too risky . . . when I got somethin' else in mind."

"Oh, this again."

"Yep, this again." The girl picked up her

plate and Miller's, went over to some loose gravel between the fire and Hawk, and scraped a handful of the gravel and dirt over one of the plates, cleaning it.

She looked at Miller. "You know that old Apache gold mine everyone's been blabberin' about for years?"

"The one the Dutchman says he found?"

"That's the one."

"What about it?"

"I know where it is," Jodi said.

Miller gave a caustic chuff. "Oh, sure you do."

"I do." Jodi was cleaning the second plate. She flashed a quick glance at Hawk and then looked over her shoulder at Miller again. "And I been waitin' for the right man to come along to help me clean it out."

Chapter 14
Tawny Head, Black Heart

The night passed even more slowly for Hawk than the day had.

Miller hadn't given him anything to eat, and his hunger, coupled with the fact that he was battered, wet from the rain, and tied, made him feel as though he were balancing a smithy's anvil on his shoulders.

Miller and the girl had kicked out their fire and retired to their lean-to. They'd rutted again as before and then Miller got up to wander around with his rifle. Hawk had spied Apache sign the day before, and he had a feeling that the killer had, as well.

Miller walked around, looking tense. He smoked for a while along the top of the ridge above the lean-to, cupping the coal in the palm of his hand as he stared out over the canyon. Then, apparently satisfied they were alone, he came down off the ridge and sauntered over to Hawk.

"Only reason I'm keepin' you alive is

'cause I don't have to haul your smelly carcass through the desert to Tucson. If it was winter, you'd be dead."

Hawk didn't say anything. He kept his eyes straight ahead, not giving the man anything.

That seemed to rile Miller. He swept his right boot back, then hurled it forward, ramming the toe into Hawk's right thigh. The pain seared through the rogue lawman's leg, but he kept quiet and held still, staring straight ahead.

"That hurt," Miller said, chuckling. "I know it did."

He kicked out of his boots and crawled back under the lean-to.

Hawk dozed now and then but sometime around three thirty or four he awakened. He'd heard something, but he wasn't sure what. The horses were milling around faintly, edgily. He recognized the grulla's deep, almost soundless whicker.

Hawk looked around. The night was still, silent. Save for the starlight, it was a black as the inside of a glove. Something or someone was on the prowl near the camp. He could tell as much by the faint tingling at the base of his spine as from anything else.

The horses continued to sidle around,

snorting, for another half hour. And then they settled down. And the tingling at the base of Hawk's back faded, as well.

At first light, Miller crawled out from under the lean-to. He muttered something to the girl then grabbed Hawk's Henry, stumbled past Hawk, and checked the horses. He didn't return soon, so Hawk figured he'd gone out on the scout again.

The killer must have sensed something the night before, as well.

The girl gathered more wood, built a small fire, and made coffee. When the coffee was done, she brought a cup over to Hawk, and dropped to a knee beside him.

"Want some coffee?"

"No, thanks," Hawk said.

Jodi looked genuinely surprised. "Really? You don't want no *coffee*?"

"Nope."

She stared at him, brows knit together. "You sure?" She blew the steam toward him. "Don't that smell good?"

Hawk didn't say anything.

"Jesus, you're a tough son of a bitch, ain't ya?"

Still, Hawk said nothing. She stared at him, sleep in her eyes, lines from her saddle still creasing her cheek. Fine lines from her slumber stretched out from the corners of her hazel eyes. She hadn't brushed her hair but merely tucked the tangled mess behind her ears.

She'd left the first three buttons of her shirt undone, showing a bit of white chemise and the first dip of cleavage.

"I s'pose you're thinkin' I might've poisoned it," she said.

"Just don't care for any of your coffee."

"Reckon I don't blame you. Since I was tryin' to get him to kill you an' all." The girl paused, feigned a sheepish look, pooching her lips out and casting her eyes low. "Sorry about that."

Hawk gave a droll chuckle.

She raised her eyes coyly. "Hope we didn't keep you awake last night . . . with all our carryin' on."

"I slept fine."

"Really?"

"Yep."

She studied him sidelong. "Pshaw! You heard. And I bet you were wantin' some, weren't you?" She pressed her hand against his shoulder, gave him a shove. "Come on! I know I'm purty. I ain't high-hatted or nothin', but I been told I'm easy on the eyes enough times I'm startin' to believe it." She looked off. "Seem to satisfy him well enough."

She rolled her eyes to Hawk. "You wanna kill him, don't you?"

Hawk looked at her.

"Why don't you, then?"

He continued to stare at her skeptically.

"You and me could be partners, you know. I'm gonna need a tough man to help me mine the gold out of that old hole. Geronimo and his Apaches keep a close eye on things up here. The Superstitions are the home of their Thunder God, and he's a colicky cuss. He don't like intruders. That's what us white folks are — even *half-breed* white folks."

Teasingly, she placed a finger on Hawk's long wedge of a nose, and shoved his face to one side, smiling and then folding her upper teeth over her bottom lip.

A brazen one, this girl. A coquette. A tawny-headed, black-hearted coquette.

Hawk wouldn't trust her as far as he could throw her uphill against a prairie cyclone.

"What're you sayin'?" Hawk said, feigning interest.

"I'm sayin' that if you was to throw in with me, I'd make it worth your while."

She slid her shoulders back slightly, pushing her breasts out, and slid her face down close to Hawk's. He could hear the faint crackling of her lips as she broadened her coquettish smile. "You'd be a rich man and you'd have a pretty, young girl to warm your fancy bed at night. To do things to you I bet you've never even dreamed of."

"Oh?"

"Sure. And all you have to do is promise me you'd like that . . . and you'd like to be richer than your wildest dreams . . . and promise to kill Pima . . . and you're in."

"You really think that old mine is more than legend?"

"I know." She gazed at him gravely now, her bold gaze certain. "I've seen it. The old man didn't. I kept it from him because I couldn't trust him to not get drunk and gas about it to others. He'd act like it was all his, like he found it himself. I saw it early in the spring, when I got lost out here, and I've drawn a map. It's in my saddlebags."

"What about the Apaches?"

"They're a problem. We'll have to be careful. It might come to fightin'. If it does, I'd rather have you doin' the fightin' than a man like Pima."

Jodi looked away as though to make certain they were alone, and then she shook her hair back from her face and leaned even closer to Hawk, until he could smell her distinctly feminine fragrance mixed with the smoky, horsy smell of her clothes, and feel her breath against his cheek.

"Just between you and me," Jodi said, "Pima's weak. He's got a weak mind and a weak soul. You know. You heard him talkin'. And what's more, I can't trust him. He don't have no integrity. I can tell by lookin' at you, though, that you got integrity. You wouldn't double-cross a girl who only wanted you to kill the man you already wanted to kill yourself and make you rich and give herself to you for an added reward."

She brushed her nose against Hawk's jaw, and smiled.

"Would you?" she asked.

Hawk gazed at her, lifted his mouth corners slightly. He glanced down her shirt because he knew she wanted him to, and then he broadened his smile and narrowed his eyes lustily. "No, I wouldn't."

"We got a deal, then?"

"Deal."

The girl stared at him skeptically, considering. And then she reached into her pants pocket. Hawk had just finished using the rock behind him to grind through the rope around his wrists, and now he swung both arms forward, showing her his hands.

"No need for the knife. But I will take a gu—"

Miller's voice cut him off. *"Hey — what the hell's goin' on over there?"*

Hawk turned to see Miller running toward him on the left, climbing the rise and holding Hawk's rifle across his hips.

"Hey!" Miller shouted as he started up the rocks toward the camp.

The girl looked from Hawk's freed hands to Miller and screamed, "Pima, help!" She dropped the coffee cup and scrambled back away from the prisoner.

The rogue lawman lunged for her, intending to grab her around her neck and take the pistol she usually carried wedged against the small of her back. But Hawk's ankles were still tied, restricting his movements, and his fingers only brushed the girl's chest before he fell forward on his belly.

Miller's boots thudded. His spurs rattled. Hawk could hear the man's raspy breaths as he ran up the rocks. Hawk turned his head in time to see the killer standing over him, boots spread, glaring down and raising the Henry, barrel up.

"I was just tryin' to give him a cup of coffee!" Jodi screamed, feigning horror.

"Why, you son of a bitch!" Miller raked out just before he rammed the brass butt plate of the rifle against Hawk's right cheek.

One more smack with the Henry laid the

rogue lawman out cold.

He didn't know how much later he woke. All he knew was that for a seemingly endless time his slumber had been racked with a searing pain in his head. It had felt — still felt — like someone had sunk a hatchet through his skull. His belly and hips ached and burned. Making the pain in his head worse, all his blood had seemed to pool in his brain, feeding the tender nerves.

His heart was two giant bells tolling wickedly in his ears.

As he opened his eyes, he saw the ground passing in a brown blur beneath him. The rich, warm tang of horse and leather filled his nostrils. He looked around. He'd been thrown belly down over his own saddle, across the grulla's back. That was the grinding he felt against his midsection. His wrists were tied even tighter than before.

His ankles were also tied and hung down the grulla's opposite side.

As he rode, gritting his teeth against the clanging in his head, Hawk heard the girl and Miller talking, one of them leading the grulla. The girl was acting as though Hawk had jumped her. She was insisting Miller kill him and "get him out of their hair for good."

They wouldn't need the reward money.

Not with all the gold waiting for them in that old Mexican mine.

Miller obviously, wisely, didn't trust her much more than Hawk did. The killer wanted to keep Hawk alive until he was certain the mine was real and not just one of Jodi's stories or a figment of her "tawny-headed imagination."

Hawk had to grin through his pain at that.

And then he saw his opportunity to get shed of these two.

They were traversing a razorback ridge. Just beyond him, a deep canyon dropped nearly straight down. What the hell? He couldn't be in any more pain than he was already in.

And he doubted he'd ever get another chance to free himself, another chance at hunting Miller down and killing him.

What was the worst that could happen?

That he'd join his waiting family?

Hawk laughed soundlessly.

With a low groan, Hawk funneled every ounce of his remaining strength into his arms and legs. He pitched and bobbed until he'd worked his knees up onto the grulla's back.

"Be seein' you, old pard," he muttered to the horse as, using his knees and elbows, he hurled himself into a somersault off the horse's back and into the canyon.

As he tumbled down the steep, shale-carpeted slope, he realized he'd been wrong. There was a whole other world of pain just waiting for him at the bottom of that canyon, grinning its snaggle-toothed grin.

Chapter 15
Torment Canyon

"How you feelin', sugar?"

It was the voice of Saradee Jones — intimate and lilting, faintly raspy and familiar to Hawk's ears. The outlaw girl's voice spoke to him from far away, as though from the top of the very deep well at the bottom of which he lay.

Of course, it wasn't really Saradee speaking to him. He was only dreaming the voice as he'd dreamt the voices of Linda and Jubal, whispering into his ears, urging him to let go. To release this world of aching torment and endless grief, and to walk with them over the green fields of their new home.

Where they would live together in serenity throughout eternity.

"Feelin' better? Why, I do believe you're still kickin', after all."

Saradee's voice. Or his mind's fabrication of her voice. She wouldn't be in this canyon.

They'd parted ways back in his hometown of Crossroads. She'd sensed, rightly, that he'd wanted to visit the graves of Linda and Jubal alone. He hadn't seen her after that visit, had no idea where she'd gone. That wasn't unusual. Their partings had always been spontaneous and without formality, just like their infrequent liaisons.

They were not partners. At least, in Hawk's mind they were not. A few months ago, she'd saved his life in a town called Trinity Ridge, when he'd been hanged upside down from a burning gallows by the Tierney Gang, and he supposed he was beholden to her for that.

But for no other reason. She was an outlaw and a killer. Someday soon, he would kill her.

Someone touched his shoulder, jostled him slightly. Her voice again. It was starting to annoy him because it was drawing him up out of the deep well of sleep again, and away from his misery. He wanted to remain deep inside the well. He felt that rising from it would only return him to an unbearable world of pain — one that he could feel hammering at him as though on the other side of a stout, log door.

The pain was like a pack of hungry wolves yapping and howling outside that door.

"Hey, Hawk," Saradee said. Close now. Very close. Her lips seemed to be just off his left ear. "Haw-awwk," she said in her lilting singsong.

He opened his eyes, squinted against the pain that was like a railroad spike hammered through both ears. What his eyes finally focused on was something shiny. Shiny silver. A cross dangling from a rawhide thong down a girl's neck, resting atop a deep well of dark cleavage exposed by the first few buttons of a well-filled hickory shirt.

The girl's neck and chest were lightly tanned. At the first downward slope of the cleavage, on the far side of the little valley from Hawk's face, was a single, jagged-edged, whiskey-colored freckle.

"Hey," the girl said. "Quit starin' at my tits. How 'bout some water?" She jostled a hide-wrapped canteen; Hawk could hear the water sloshing around.

And then he realized how thirsty he was and that he'd been dreaming of snowmelt — of diving into a snowmelt stream and letting the water flow into his mouth, down his throat, and into his belly.

Hawk lifted his head, which he then realized was being held up by the girl's right shoulder. She lifted the canteen across her well-filled blouse and the silver crucifix nestling at the top of her cleavage, shoving the flask toward his mouth. But Hawk found himself raising his right arm and wrapping that hand around the canteen, taking it from her.

He tipped up the canteen, pressed the metal ring of the opening to his lips, and drank thirstily.

"Easy, fella," Saradee said as water dribbled down the corners of Hawk's mouth. "It's been three days. You drink too much too soon, you'll founder."

Hawk couldn't help himself. The water tasted too good. He pulled the canteen away from his mouth, filled his now-thirsty lungs with air, and then let the water wash down his throat once more, filling his belly. Instantly, it buoyed him, made him feel better. He was like a plant that had gone too long without water.

On the other hand, for some reason, that hammering at his door now seeped through an opening, rapping that railroad spike from both ends. He hardened his jaws, gritted his teeth, pulled away from the girl, and leaned his head back against a wall.

"Hell!"

"Yeah, well, I told ya," Saradee said, taking the canteen from him. "You oughta listen to Saradee. She's here to help . . . just like always."

"Where in the hell am I?" Hawk said, dragging a ragged breath into his lungs.

He felt a strange pressure around his head and reached up to feel a bandanna tightly wrapped around his forehead and tied in back. His fingers touched crusted blood at the front and back.

Only then did he remember his tumble down the steep slope into the canyon — the raking, hammering pain in every joint, sharp rocks and cactus thorns biting into him.

"Found this old shack," Saradee said, looking around. "I think the canyon's called Torment. Leastways, it says that on an old map I took out of the stage station. I reckon that would be fitting under the circumstances, wouldn't it?"

Hawk looked around. Stone walls, mostly ruined, rose around him. There was a brush roof over his head, but most of the roof of the small casa — probably an ancient Mexican rancher's or herder's hovel — had tumbled into the barren rooms. The floor was hard-packed desert caliche.

Outside, the sun shone brightly off barren rock. A hot breeze slid a catclaw's branches back and forth in a far window. The

186

branches scraped softly against the old stone.

A saddle and other tack lay on the floor around him. There was a fire ring mounded with gray ashes and a charred cedar branch. A coffeepot sat to one side, as did several other eating utensils, pots and pans.

Saradee's gear.

Her words had been slow to penetrate his brain. Now, as they did, he turned to her sitting close beside him. "Stage station?"

"Superstition. Shadowed you there." She huddled close to him, wrapped her hands around his left bicep. "Just can't seem to get shed of me, can you?"

He stared at her, gave a wry chuff. He wasn't surprised that she'd followed him. He wasn't sure what she wanted from him. She seemed amused by him, somehow. Amused by his venomous quest for vengeance. It seemed to attract her, keep her dogging his heels, as though she were mesmerized by his single-mindedness.

She was no more capable of love than he was, so he knew she didn't love him. He had to admit feeling something for her, though.

More than *something*.

A insatiable hunger for her body, which, young, ripe, and supple, was impossible for any man to ignore. And once he'd fallen prey to this blonde-haired, blue-eyed succubus's bewitching wiles, the man found himself thinking about her almost constantly.

At least, when he wasn't thinking about killing.

"You followed me into the mountains."

Saradee sighed and let her hands flop against her thighs clad in skintight, light-blue denim under leather chaps. "Search me why I came. You'd think I'd have outgrown you by now, gone back to bank- and train-robbin', cold-blooded murder and my sundry other wicked ways. But when I saw you pull through Albacurk, I just couldn't help but dog you, see what kind of bailiwick you ended up in next."

She squirmed against him, kissed his cheek. Her sun-bleached blonde hair hung straight and long past her slender shoulders. It fell down both sides of her doll-like face bejeweled with the long, deep-blue eyes of an outlaw sorceress. They were crazy, taunting, eminently alluring eyes — even crazier and more taunting than Jodi Zimmerman's eyes.

She was similar to the other young outlaw woman whose path Hawk had recently crossed. But even Miss Zimmerman could learn a whole book of unspeakable lessons from the outlaw queen known as Saradee Jones, whom some said *acted* like a witch because she indeed *was* a witch.

An outlaw witch.

Pity the poor fool who let her sink her bittersweet claws into him, as Gideon Hawk had made the mistake of doing himself. Every time he laid eyes on Saradee, he rued the day he hadn't killed her before she could lure him into her bed.

Now, since she'd somehow saved his hide again — or, at least gotten a roof over his head and doctored his wounds — he knew he should be glad that he hadn't drilled a bullet through her beautiful head. But he just couldn't manage it.

Hawk found himself staring at her in disbelief at both her beauty, the pureness of which belied her malevolence, and the fact of her presence.

"That was you I sensed around Miller's camp last night, wasn't it?" Hawk said.

"I was workin' around you, tryin' to figure a way to get you out of there. Wasn't in much of a hurry, I reckon. I was kinda wondering if that randy little bitch, Miss Jodi, was going to lure you into the trap she was settin'."

Hawk chuckled as he grabbed the canteen

out of her hands. "You must've been close."
He threw back another deep drink.

Saradee snatched the canteen back from
him. "You wanna founder?"

She returned the cap to the canteen's
mouth and said, "I was scoutin' from across
the canyon when you pulled that fool move,
throwin' yourself off your horse. You fell a
ways but you might've fallen farther. Got
hung up on a ledge of sorts. Miller was going to shoot you but the girl — she's a smart
one, ain't she? — she knocked his rifle away.
Must've reminded him of the Apache dan-
ger. I reckon they figured you were a goner,
anyway, so they moved on. I had a devil of
a time gettin' you off that ledge and hauled
into the canyon. Rigged a travois, dragged
you around lookin' for shelter, found this
place."

Saradee appraised their surroundings.

"It ain't much, but it's been home now
for the past three days. I reckon it's grown
on me. Don't recollect stayin' in one place
this long in a month of Sundays."

"Three days, huh?"

"Three days. I bet you gotta pee like a
plow horse!"

It was then that Hawk realized he was
naked beneath a coarse army blanket. He
lifted the blanket. Aside from a large ban-

dage cut from a blanket wrapped taut around his ribs, and another couple of bandages wrapped around cuts on his legs, he was as naked as the day he'd been born.

Saradee had even taken off his socks.

She laughed. "Don't worry, sugar — I've seen it before." She winked at him.

Hawk cursed. Not because he was naked, but from the general wretchedness of his situation. Little modesty remained in him. He flung the blanket aside, heaved himself slowly, heavily to his feet, setting his jaws against the hammering in his head, and stumbled barefoot and naked out of the shack. A few feet beyond the front door, he evacuated his bladder on a prickly pear.

Saradee's big palomino stood hobbled nearby, in a patch of shade between a couple of mesquites growing among the rocks. The horse lowered its head, whickered softly at the naked man watering the prickly pear. Hawk looked around, saw that they were in a slight bowl surrounded by low, barren hills.

Almost straight to the west rose the finger-like formation of what was most likely the peak called Weaver's Needle. Some old prospectors called it by its Spanish name, El Sombrero.

The sun was blinding. That, coupled with

the shrill, pulsating music of the cicadas, caused the ground to rise and fall around Hawk. He suddenly felt sick to his stomach. He grabbed the doorframe to steady himself but, twisting around, he dropped to his knees anyway.

Saradee was there beside him, draping one of his arms around her neck, wrapping her own arm around his waist.

"Easy does it, sugar!" Saradee said, grunting against the big man's considerable weight.

Hawk got his feet under him but his knees felt like wheel dope. He leaned against the girl but his knees were grazing the ground by the time she got him back to the crude pallet she'd made for him over leafy willow branches and burlap. Hawk lay down in the makeshift bed. He tried fighting against the nausea and the infernal swimming in his head, the pounding in his temples, but it was no use.

Outside, thunder rumbled. He glanced toward the doorway, saw the white-hot light dim slightly. Another summer storm was moving in.

More thunder rumbled like distant war drums. Hawk took that as a sign to give into his own weakness and the pressure of Saradee's hands pushing him down, and flopped back against the pallet.

He was asleep before his head had hit the saddlebag pouch that the outlaw girl had filled with sand for his pillow.

When he opened his eyes, it was dark. A small fire burned nearby. It shone in Linda's yellow-blonde hair as, straddling him naked, she rose and fell slowly, gently grinding against him. He looked down to see his wife's hands with her gold wedding band pressed against his chest. As she lifted her hips, she leaned forward, pushing comfortingly against him. As she dropped back down to his pelvis, the pressure on his chest lightened.

Hawk smiled. He was home. His smile broadened. His pain was gone. There was only Linda making love to him, her long hair obscuring her face as it cascaded down her shoulders to caress his chest, soft as corn silk, when she leaned forward.

"Oh, Gid," she whispered. "Oh . . . Gideon . . ."

Behind her now in the firelight he could see the basinet in which their baby, little Jubal, slumbered among the quilts she'd sewn for him during her pregnancy.

Hawk lifted his hands to his wife's breasts, gently massaging the full, high, cherry-tipped orbs before caressing her cheeks with his thumbs. He slid her hair back from her face with the backs of his hands.

Hawk froze, staring up at the girl straddling him.

It was not Linda's soft, light-blue eyes smiling down at him now but the glassy, nearly opaque, folly-ridden gaze of Saradee Jones.

The beautiful outlaw shook her head slowly, stretching her rich lips back from her white teeth in gentle mockery. "Not her, Gideon. Linda's dead. She's back in one of those two graves you visited back in Crossroads — remember?"

Saradee lowered her hips to his and then bowed her head and tightened her face as she ground against him, groaning hoarsely. "Just me now. Just . . . ohhh, god . . . *me*!"

Hawk tried in his mind to resist her. He could not.

His blood rose undeniably. He grunted and cupped her breasts almost savagely and drove himself up deep inside her. He pressed the back of his head fast against the blankets, cursing and squeezing her breasts as he spent himself.

Saradee sighed and collapsed against his chest.

Outside, the palomino whinnied.

Then came the thuds of many galloping horses.

Saradee gasped. As she flung her naked, sweat-slick body off of Hawk, he reached for his Henry.

CHAPTER 16
IN THUNDER GOD'S ABODE

Hawk had automatically gone for his rifle, which he'd assumed was lying where he usually kept it, to the right of his bedroll. He'd forgotten that he'd taken his leave of Miller and Jodi Zimmerman without any weapons save for the dagger he kept in his boot.

He'd remembered too late that his rifle was still with Miller. The quick, twisting move had grieved his battered ribs. As he gave an agonized grunt and pressed his right hand to his side, he heard the thunder of several horses outside the ruined hovel.

Naked, Saradee turned to Hawk.

"Here!" she hissed, and tossed him one of her silver-chased, pearl-gripped Colts.

Hawk caught the weapon against his chest. Saradee quickly threw her shirt over her shoulders and ran to the outline of a window to Hawk's left. The fire had burned down to a soft, umber glow, leaving the hovel in thick, inky shadows lightly limned in red.

Hawk spun the Colt's cylinder and, rising heavily but vaguely realizing he wasn't in as much pain as before, he moved to a window on the opposite side of the cabin from Saradee. He hunkered on one knee to the left of the empty casing and gazed out into the dark canyon.

Hooves thumped. Horses whickered softly, occasionally blowing. There was also the rasping of men. For a moment, Hawk could see nothing out there, only hear the horses and the men who seemed to be circling the hovel. But then as his eyes adjusted to the night's moonless darkness, Hawk saw the quick-moving shadows maybe thirty, forty yards out from the shack.

Occasionally, starlight reflected off a face or an eye or some metallic object that the riders carried. Briefly, between two shrubs, Hawk glimpsed a patch of red. Likely a calico bandanna — the kind favored by Apaches. He could tell from the muffled hoof thuds that the horses galloping around the hovel were unshod, another sign that Apaches — likely, Chiricahuas — had come calling.

Hawk felt the chill of apprehension seep into his battered body. Out of the frying pan and into the fire. And he had neither his own pistols nor his Henry repeater. Just Saradee's Colt, which left her with maybe only one more Colt and her Winchester.

How many Indians were out there?

Hunkered down beside the window and staring out into the night, he tried to count the shadows swirling around him. They seemed to be moving at a fairly good clip on their sure-footed, desert- and mountain-bred mustangs — too fast for Hawk to get a handle on their number.

He waited, his thumb caressing the cocked hammer of Saradee's Colt. He hadn't realized how hard he'd been clamping his jaws together until they started to hurt. His palm grew slick against the Colt's pearl grips.

Movement behind Hawk. He turned to see Saradee leap the fire and run toward him. Light from the umber coals bathed her bare legs, glistened in her blonde hair and her eyes. She hunkered down on the opposite side of the window from Hawk. He could sense her anxiety as the riders continued circling.

"Injuns!" she hissed.

"Hold your fire."

"I'll hold mine if they hold theirs!"

Hawk continued staring out the window. The riders continued circling, jangling

Hawk's nerves just as he knew they were doing to Saradee's. He had the urge to dress but he didn't want to turn his back on them. Besides, it wasn't cold and he might as well die naked as clothed.

Give the carrion eaters an easier time of it.

Just when Hawk thought he couldn't endure the tension any longer, the hoof thuds began to dwindle. Fewer and fewer shadows passed outside the window. Then one more passed, and that was all. The hoof thuds dwindled into the night.

Silence.

"What the hell?" Saradee said.

"Might be a trap."

Hawk rose and stiffly gathered his clothes. Even more stiffly, he wrestled his way into his longhandles, whipcord trousers, socks, and boots. He pulled his suspenders up over his longhandle top. Again, he looked for his rifle. It was so much a part of him, he felt as though one of his arms had been hacked off at the shoulder.

He tossed Saradee's Colt her to her, and picked up her Winchester carbine. She preferred pistols. He preferred a long gun. He racked a shell into the Winchester's chamber and then, thumb on the hammer, walked slowly out into the night.

In front of the door, he stopped and looked around. He did not hear Saradee move out of the shack behind him. She was as stealthy as a night-hunting puma. He only felt the slight displacement of air as she stepped up beside him. She smelled like cinnamon and the musk of love.

Hawk canted his head to his left. The girl drifted off that way. Hawk moved to his right. He didn't know the terrain like she did, so he had to move especially slowly and carefully so he wouldn't trip and give himself away or walk into an ambush.

When he figured he'd moved about fifty yards out from the canyon, he stared off in the direction in which he was sure the Indians had headed. West. Nothing but silence out there in the stygian darkness, save for the distant yammer of a lone coyote.

Saradee's voice cleaved the silence. "Hawk."

He turned and walked back toward the shack. He stopped when he saw the cream figure of the big palomino fidgeting around the mesquite it had been tied to. Saradee stood several yards behind the horse. Some slender object slanted down before her.

Hawk moved toward her and saw the feathers trimming the wooden shaft pro-truding from the ground behind the palomino. An Apache war lance.

"What the hell's that mean?" the girl said, her voice pitched low with gravity.

"It means get out or they'll escort us out . . . by way of hell."

Hawk turned and walked back to the shack.

"You know, I think I'll kill you for lyin' to me, girl!"

Pima Miller glared at Jodi Zimmerman, who, sitting on her Morgan mare in one of the many shallow canyons that formed a maze in the heart of the Superstitions, turned her head this way and that. Her brows hooded her troubled eyes, and her lips were stretched, balling her cheeks in a frustrated scowl.

"I don't understand it," she said, glancing down at the penciled scrap of paper in her gloved hands. "I was careful to write down the directions and draw clear pictures of the terrain. I knew I'd have trouble finding it if I didn't, and —"

"And now, even with your map, you're still havin' trouble findin' it. And we've been out here for three days now. Three long days in this heat followin' your so-called map and your so-called *story* of the richest gold mine in all of North America."

"Oh, hush — I'm tryin' to figure."

"Tryin' to figure, huh? I'm tryin' to figure what in the hell ever got into me to listen to your wild story in the first place. Now, not only do I not have a pair of saddlebags bulgin' with nearly pure gold ore, but I don't have that rogue lawman's head in a gunnysack!" Miller wagged his head from side to side, groaning. "Did I say that head of his is worth twenty thousand dollars? Did I *say* that?"

"I believe you might've mentioned it among all your other caterwauling," Jodi said, holding the map in front of her but looking back over her left shoulder at the large, red pinnacle of El Sombrero.

The formation did indeed resemble a sombrero from this vantage — the steeple crown of the hat rising from a stark, red, boulder-strewn, cone-like mountain and presiding over the entire Superstition Range and the Salt River Valley, with the airy blue backdrop of Boulder Canyon to the southwest.

The vastness and starkness of the land here always took Jodi's breath away. It made her feel at once lonely and anxious but, also, knowing the ancient mine that the land contained, like a jewel clamped in the palm of a giant fist, it made her giddy and eager.

It made her heart tap-tap-tap-tap, like an Apache war drum, in her throat, in her ears.

But, now, if she couldn't find it, knowing that she'd been so infernally close, maybe within only two hundred yards after waiting for the old man to die or for her to work up the gumption to leave him behind and ride out here alone and chip off what she could from the precious jewel and then head for far, far better climes — the disappointment would be a bottomless well.

She'd never stop falling into it.

If she couldn't find the old Peralta mine, she'd put her pistol in her mouth and blow her brains out.

How could anyone go on living, knowing the riches they'd left behind? She'd seen it! After the Dutchman from Apache Springs had left with his two burros, she'd back-tracked him, found the mine and explored it, seen the color in the walls.

It had been like the scales of a giant diamondback fashioned from raw, glittering gold!

Jodi was sweating. It was running down her cheeks, between her breasts and down her shoulders under her shirt. Her breath was short and shallow. The cicadas were screeching a raucous, throbbing rhythm that matched the throbbing of the girl's own heart.

Desperately, she looked around. There were several lesser canyons, most brush- and rock-choked, angling away from this main one they were in and which was maybe fifty yards across at its widest. The old man had said these ravines were old lava rivers from the time the Superstitions had been created by exploding volcanoes.

She glanced back over the rumpled, barren land to the southwest and El Sombrero, and then "Tsucked" her horse on ahead, looking around for some of the landmarks she'd carefully penciled on her sheet of lined notepaper.

"You best find that gold, girl."

Behind her, Miller stepped down from his saddle and removed his canteen from the horn. He was leading Hawk's grulla. They figured they'd use the rogue lawman's mount and his saddlebags for squirreling out an extra parcel of the Dutchman's gold from the mine.

"You best find it . . ." Miller let his voice taper off maliciously as he walked over to the shaded base of the arroyo's western bank, and sagged down with a grunt. "Me — I'm gonna rest here, have me some water. I think your stitches done opened up on me."

Jodi looked behind her again. She could see a little splotch of fresh blood on the outlaw's shirt.

She lifted her gaze to the red sandstone ridges rising all around her. She'd spied Apache sign the day before, and she thought she'd sensed the red men following them, staying just out of sight. It was said that Geronimo saw himself as a keeper of the Superstitions, so to speak. The Chiricahuas had long called the mountains their physical as well as spiritual home. It was also the home of their Thunder God.

Geronimo, as did Cochise before him, wanted to keep the mountains free of the white-eyes. The Apaches haunting these mountains didn't kill as automatically and wantonly as they once had, fearing retribution from the cavalry, but gold hunters were still known to disappear in these mountains, never to be heard from again.

Somehow, the old Dutchman, as well as Jodi and the old man, had managed to steer clear of the dangerous Chiricahuas. Her time was likely running out, she thought as she continued to rake her gaze around the rocky ridges for sign of the little, dark, savage men with their coal-black hair held back by calico headbands.

The Morgan moved steadily north along

the ravine. The sun shifted across the sky, angling westward. Shadows slithered along the wash and along the crags. As one particular shadow edged along the top of a boulder rising along the ravine's eastern bank, it revealed something.

Jodi looked at the map in her hands, its corners ruffling in the dry breeze.

Her heart hiccupped as she slid her gaze from the rock drawn on the map to the actual boulder rising on the eastern bank. When she saw the ancient drawing painted on the boulder's upper right corner in ochre — a stick man on foot facing down some large, round, bear-like creature with a long lance — she had to purse her lips to hold back a scream.

A smile exploding across her face, she looked back at Miller who sat against the bank, his canteen beside him, one knee raised, running a wet handkerchief back and forth across his hatless head.

"I found it!" she hissed. "Bring the horses! I found it!"

The outlaw looked at her, his mouth open, his ginger-bearded, narrow-eyed face turned sunset red by the sun. "Huh?"

Jodi beckoned broadly. "Hurry, you damn fool — I found it!"

CHAPTER 17
THE STRANGER

Hawk pressed his back against the escarpment and set his boots a little farther than shoulder-width apart. He was in the shade here in this rocky corridor, but the air was still as hot as the hobbs of hell. As he heard footsteps approaching from the boulder's other side, he told himself it was about to get hotter.

He held Saradee's carbine barrel up in front of him. The Winchester was cocked, and his right index finger was curled against the trigger, ready.

The soft, crunching falls of moccasin-clad feet stopped. A sweat bead dribbled down from Hawk's right sideburn to his jawline. He frowned, squeezing the Winchester in his hands.

Why had the brave stopped?

Then he glimpsed movement in the corner of his right eye. He turned to see a dark head wrapped in red calico and a pair of black eyes staring at him from over the top of a boulder on the other side of the ravine down which the first brave had been coming. The first brave had apparently been warned to hold his ground by the one atop the boulder who just now slid his cheek against the neck of the Winchester he was aiming at the rogue lawman.

Hawk threw himself forward against another boulder as the Apache's Winchester coughed shrilly, smoke and red flames leaping from the barrel. The slug slammed into the rock against which Hawk had pressed his back a moment before.

Shards and rock dust flew.

Hawk raised his own carbine and fired at the Indian atop the rock, who was suddenly no longer there, and then he stepped out from the gap between boulders he'd been hunkered in. The Apache whose footsteps Hawk had been hearing was just around the corner. Hawk's sudden appearance caused the brave to snap his eyes wide and trigger the carbine he was aiming straight out from his left hip.

Hawk triggered his own rifle a quarter second later. The staccato blasts echoed shrilly together. The Chiricahua's bullet hammered the boulder flanking Hawk, maybe two inches off the rogue lawman's right hip, while Hawk's slug took the brave in the gut.

The brave leaped dramatically back, as though from a coiled snake, his carbine dangling in his left hand, barrel aimed at the ground. His molasses-colored eyes flashed at Hawk as he tried to reset his feet, but then Hawk shot him again, in the forehead.

The second bullet lifted the young, stocky brave with tattoos on the insides of his cherry-brown arms, straight up and back and threw him onto the ground that Hawk's slug had painted with the red and white contents of the young warrior's skull.

Instantly, Hawk wheeled toward the boulder atop which he'd seen the other brave. The rogue lawman's second spent cartridge wheeled over his right shoulder to clatter onto the ground behind him as he pumped a live round into the chamber.

He stared at the boulder, skidding his gaze from side to side and to the top. And then, not seeing his target, he ran across the narrow ravine and along the boulder's left side. He continued running straight out behind it, stopping suddenly and wheeling to his right, expecting to see the brave hunkered down behind the privy-sized chunk of black lava.

"Hawk!" It was Saradee's voice behind him.

Hawk wheeled as a pistol popped. Ten yards behind Hawk, the second brave lowered the Spencer repeater he'd been aiming at Hawk. The Chiricahua stumbled forward on the toes of his moccasins, the fire in his eyes dying fast. He dropped the Spencer as he twisted around to see Saradee aiming one of her silver-chased Colts, gray smoke curling from the barrel.

Movement behind Saradee.

"Down!" Hawk shouted.

The girl dropped like a fifty-pound sack of cracked corn as Hawk snapped his carbine to his shoulder. Hawk fired and watched the brave who'd been coming up behind the blonde, nocking an arrow to an ash bow, fire the fletched arrow into the ground at his feet and then twist around and stagger back in the opposite direction before dropping to his knees.

He gave a guttural cry as he tried to heave himself to his feet, but then he stumbled forward and fell belly down on the ground, quivering as the life left him. Saradee, also lying belly down, lifted her wide-eyed face toward Hawk, glanced behind at the brave who'd almost perforated her pretty hide with a razor-edged strap-iron arrow point.

She turned back toward Hawk and grinned.

Hawk walked back the way he'd just come, looking around carefully. He gazed up and down the ravine before crossing it and crouching down beside the first brave he'd shot. The brave was carrying a Winchester repeater outfitted with a leather lanyard trimmed with filled cartridge loops. Kicking the dead warrior over, Hawk also found that he carried a Schofield .44 behind a red cotton sash.

Hawk slung the brave's Winchester over his own right shoulder, and pulled the Schofield out of the sash. He tripped the latch and broke open the top-break pistol. All six chambers showed brass. Hawk snapped the revolver closed and snugged it into one of his two empty holsters — the one he wore in the cross-draw position on his left hip.

Saradee moved up behind him. He saw her shadow slide along the red, rocky ground. She was looking around cautiously. Softly, she said, "Any more?"

"Hell if I know." Hawk held out the carbine he'd borrowed. "Here."

Saradee looked at her rifle and then at the one hanging from Hawk's shoulder as well as the Schofield in his holster. Her cheeks dimpled and she shook her blonde hair back from her face. "You're racking up."

"Now, I just need a horse."

They'd left the ancient shack Hawk had been healing in two days ago. They'd had to ride double on Saradee's palomino as Hawk continued his hunt for Pima Miller. The palomino was strong, but the heat and extra weight were taking its toll, slowing them down.

Hawk needed a horse. Even if it wasn't his own grulla. Any horse would do. Even a half-broken Chiricahua mustang that likely didn't care for the smell of white men.

Or anything else about white men . . .

Hawk and Saradee had spied the Indians milling along a ridge about an hour ago, around three in the hot afternoon. Sensing an ambush, Hawk had decided to bring the ambush to the Chiricahuas. True, he and Saradee were the interlopers here. The Apaches were only protecting what they believed to be theirs, a mountain of religious significance — their Thunder God's abode. But Hawk doubted they'd mind if he didn't sell his life cheaply.

A true Chiricahua would not flinch at a mortal challenge.

The next challenge for Hawk was to secure one of the warriors' horses.

He made sure his new carbine was fully

loaded and then he looked around. He sensed that the Indians had come from the north, so he stepped out into the ravine and stared in that direction.

Spying no more imminent threats, he glanced at Saradee. "Fetch your horse."

"Whatever you say, lover."

"Stop callin' me that," Hawk said, angrily squeezing his new carbine's neck as he looked around at the weird pinnacles and glyphs of rock rising in all directions.

"Don't give me orders . . . *lover.*" Saradee looked around warily. "Are you sure Miller is worth all this? Maybe you should find another killer to kill. One who hasn't embedded himself so deep in *Apacheria.*"

The sun was hammering down on Hawk, who had lost his hat sometime before Miller and the Zimmerman girl had thrown him over his horse. Now he went back to the Apache, removed the strip of calico banding the young warrior's head, and wrapped it around his own.

As he tied the cloth in back, he said, "You can leave whenever you want. You never had to ride out here in the first place."

Hawk meant it. He didn't like having her around. Or was it that he liked having her around *too much*?

She smiled at him, reached up to adjust

the calico bandanna on his forehead. She'd dimpled her pretty, suntanned cheeks again. A few strands of her hair, sun-bleached nearly white, blew against his cheek. He felt the raw pull of her deep in his loins.

Her infernal pull.

"Leave and miss out on all this fun?" Saradee shook her head. "Not a chance, lover. I'll fetch my horse."

She turned and strode away. Hawk couldn't help watching her go, admiring the sway of her full, firm hips and round ass strained against her light-blue denims. Her chaps slapped against her long, slender legs as she walked, silver spurs ringing lightly.

Her hair slid back and forth along her slender back, blowing out from her face in the hot, dry breeze.

Hawk turned away from her and continued walking along the ravine. He saw the light indentations that the Apaches' moccasins had made in the caliche. He followed them into an off-shooting canyon and then into an open, sandy area. He stopped in a wedge of shade, and snapped up the Winchester.

Three horses milled in the chaparral to Hawk's left. Paint Indian ponies with simple hemp hackamores and colorful Apache blankets for saddles. He was glad to see the horses but what had him riveted was the white man staked back-down to a slight rise ahead and on Hawk's right.

Hawk looked around the man, making sure he wasn't walking into a trap. When he deemed himself alone, with only the staked man for company, Hawk moved forward. He stopped at the base of the slope to which the man had been staked.

The man was groaning and turning his head from side to side, squeezing his eyes shut against the sun. He stopped moving and his eyelids flickered as he tried to see through them.

"Someone there?" To Hawk, his Old World accent sounded German. His dark-brown beard, lightly threaded with gray, hung to the middle of his chest clad in a sweat-matted, salt-stained buckskin shirt. A hide tobacco pouch hung down his chest, half-concealed by his beard.

Hawk looked around carefully and then moved up the slope to stare down at the gent. The man squinted up at Hawk. He must have seen only Hawk's dark hair and the red bandanna, for he spat out, "Miserable savages! Kill me and get it over with!" Then he grunted out several angry words in the Chiricahua tongue.

Hawk said, "Easy. I'm not gonna kill you."

When he was relatively sure no more Indians were near, Hawk let his carbine hang down his back by the lanyard. He pulled his dagger from his right boot and cut the man's wrists free of the ironwood stakes they'd been lashed to with strips of muslin that had no doubt been looted from some white settler's ranch house or wagon.

When Hawk had freed both the man's wrists, he reached down to cut loose his ankles. "How many were there?" he asked, still looking around. The only sign of the Indians were the three contentedly grazing mustangs.

The man had sat up. He was eyeing Hawk suspiciously. He had dark-brown eyes set deep in dark sockets, and a lean, weathered face. "Five jumped me," he said in a deep voice, rubbing each wrist in turn. "Somehow the devils snuck up on me. Strange. I've done good, skinnin' clear of 'em."

He seemed deeply baffled by the attack, as though he were fairly confident in his ability to avoid the Apaches.

Hawk said, "That means there's two more around here somewhere."

The man shook his head as his second ankle came free of the stake. He wore high-topped, lace-up boots, his buckskin trousers stuffed into them. Both trouser knees were

216

patched, the patches nearly worn through to his longhandles.

"They come runnin' through here a few minutes ago," the man, who Hawk assumed was a prospector, said, glancing off toward a relatively flat stretch of rocky, brush-speckled desert to the north. "Apaches don't like a fight unless it's a sure thing."

Hawk stared to the north. He used a hand to shade his eyes. He thought he could make out two figures bobbing in the hazy, brassy distance, heading toward a distant, copper-colored, shelving ridge.

Hawk looked at the prospector. The man was studying Hawk closely, his brown eyes still skeptical. Hawk extended his hand and tried a reassuring smile.

"Hawk," he said.

The prospector had an addled air. Hawk wasn't sure if it was from the attack or if he was just naturally edgy, suspicious of strangers. Something told him it was the latter.

The man slowly closed his own hand around Hawk's. He was not wearing a glove, but it felt like he was. His palm was so thoroughly calloused that if felt like a glove liberally crusted with dried mud.

He did not give his name, merely nodded slightly, one eye twitching, and then looked away. He gained his feet heavily. He was tall and broad-shouldered, potbellied, bandy-legged. He brushed dust from his trousers, picked up a canvas hat lying nearby, set it on his head, and began tramping off to the north.

"Fetch my burros," he muttered just loudly enough for Hawk to hear. He hacked up phlegm, spat to one side, and kept walking.

Hawk stared after him. Saradee put her palomino up beside the rogue lawman and stared off toward the north, lifting a gloved hand to her hat brim, shading her eyes.

"Who's that?"

"Hell if I know," Hawk said.

CHAPTER 18
GOLD!

"I can't believe this," Miller heard himself mutter. "I can't . . . I can't believe this. I must be feverish . . . *dreamin'*!"

On his knees, he used a hammer to chip at the scale-like lumps of gold in the mine's low ceiling. He closed his eyes and lowered his head as the gold and bits of quartz and dirt rained down on him. One chunk bounced off his hat. It smarted as it raked his forehead, but he didn't mind. In fact, he barely felt it.

Miller coughed against the dust wafting in the close, shadowy confines and looked down at the gold nugget about half the size of his fist glistening up at him in the wedge of daylight angling down from a ceiling crack farther down the hole.

The crack was just beyond where Jodi was working, filling her second set of saddlebags. She chuckled as she set down her hammer and buckled the pouch she'd just filled.

"Told ya, didn't I?" she jeered. "And you thought I was lyin'."

"I did," Miller admitted, chipping away at another nugget protruding from the ceiling above his head. "I did at that." He stopped hammering at the gold and grinned at the girl, winking. He felt so light that he thought it fully possible he might float like a feather on the wind.

Float over the earth, grinning.

"May I apologize, Miss Jodi?" the killer said. "May I do that? *Sincerely?*"

"No need to apologize," Jodi said, gaining her feet and trying to heft the saddlebags onto her shoulder. No doing. The bag was way too heavy. She'd have to drag it along the ground. "Just fill them pouches and meet me outside. We'd best head on out of here before the Dutchman pays his mine another visit."

"Pshaw!" Miller said. "Chances of him makin' another visit when we're here are slim to none."

"Just the same . . ." Jodi grunted as, crouching — the ceiling was too low for her to stand up straight — she started dragging her filled saddlebags up the slant of this secondary mine shaft. "We only have these three saddlebags . . . and three horses. No point in tarryin'."

"What a shame," Miller said. "What a damn shame we don't have one more horse. Or two horses. Two big mules. Think of that!"

"We already got enough gold here to see us through two or three lifetimes, killer. Keep your mind on that. I been all through this, dreamin' at night about drivin' a whole herd of mules up here, drive 'em out loaded with gold. But, then, shit — the Apaches would probably find me, run me down."

Jodi was grunting, breathless, as she dragged the bags up the secondary shaft to the main one, her silhouetted figure growing smaller and smaller against the light of the shaft's front entrance. "No point in gettin' greedy. We just gotta take what we can carry and get out before the Apaches or the Dutchman finds us here!"

"I ain't afraid of no Dutchman," Miller said, knocking another nugget free from the ceiling. "Ain't afraid of no Apaches, neither!"

The gold and quartz thumped onto the mineshaft floor. The floor, walls, and ceiling still showed the chips and gouges from Miguel Peralta's many peon miners who'd toiled in the mine about forty years ago. They'd exploited the main vein into the mountain, and then they must have started on the secondary shaft, near the main shaft's mouth, just before they'd heard the war drums and hightailed it.

Miller and Jodi didn't have torches so they'd penetrated the mine no farther than the light. There was plenty of gold right here for the taking, and not even hard taking at that!

So, the legend was real!

Peralta had really been here, mining the gold that Coronado had heard about. It had been Apaches who'd killed Peralta and his men when they'd fled down the mountains toward Mexico with a string of gold-laden burros.

As the burros had bolted from the gunfire and flying arrows, the gold had been scattered to the four winds.

"Plenty more where that came from," Miller said, chuckling as he worked.

"What's that?" Jodi called, crouching at the entrance about fifty yards up the shaft.

"Nothin'!" Miller said. "Just talkin' to myself! We rich men tend to that, don't ya know!"

He laughed hard at that, giddy.

Giddy.

Liable to sail off on the next low cloud . . .

"Meet ya outside!" Jodi yelled. "Don't linger. Just fill them bags and pull your picket pin!"

"Yeah, yeah," Miller said, stuffing several small chunks into a pouch of the saddlebags open near his knees on the shaft floor. "Now she's gettin' all bossy. Ain't that just the way, though?"

He chuckled some more. Jodi's bossiness didn't bother Pima Miller. Nothing bothered Miller and he doubted that anything ever would bother him again.

He chuckled at that, too, and tried to stuff another couple of small nuggets into the saddlebag pouch. He pushed and tucked and tried to break the nuggets into smaller pieces.

They just wouldn't fit.

He looked down at the nuggets in his right, gloved hand. What a shame. What a damned shame. Leaving good gold behind.

He tossed the gold chunks into the darkness farther down the shaft, heard them thump and clink as they struck the floor and rolled. That made him laugh, too. Tossing gold around as though they were mere rocks. Like he was a kid skipping stones on a quiet lake.

Hah!

Miller buckled the flap on the bulging pouch, gained his feet, and began dragging the bags on up the shaft. He groaned against the hitch in his side, where the rogue lawman had shot him. The stitches were pulling free. Miller had been feeling blood welling from the wound for the past several days.

As soon as he made it down to Tucson, he'd have to have a real sawbones stitch him up again. Now that he was rich, he couldn't take any chances on not living a good, long, full life! One hell of a rich life indeed!

Hell, he was richer than Horace Tabor! He was richer than Jay Gould and all them railroad barons back east!

Hah!

Miller dragged his saddlebags up the shaft. He had to crawl to make it easier on his side, since he couldn't stand up all the way.

By the time he'd gained the entrance, where the light momentarily blinded him and the heat blasted against him like the breath of an angry dragon, he gained his feet, slung the bags over his shoulder and made his way over to where Jodi was tightening her Morgan's saddle cinches.

One pair of bulging saddlebags hung behind her cantle. The other was on the rogue lawman's grulla.

Miller headed for Hawk's horse. It was eyeing him skeptically. The girl had fed each of the horses a pile of peeled barrel cactus, as up here at the entrance to the mine nothing grew but rocks and prickly pear.

Miller grinned at her. Even with the hundred pounds of gold on his back, he felt as light as a cottonwood leaf. "Girl, I might just let you please me extra fine tonight!"

Jodi looked at him askance. "I'd rather fuck Cochise, dead as that old Injun is."

Miller eased the saddlebags across Hawk's empty saddle and turned to her, sure he'd misunderstood or that she was just back to teasing him again. "Huh?"

"You heard me."

Jodi had tightened her cinches and now she turned toward the outlaw, leaned against the side of the black, and crossed her arms on her breasts. She looked Miller up and down, and curled a nostril. "First the old man tellin' me what to do and when to do it, and don't do that, girl, do this . . . and oh, no, you done it all wrong, girl! Makin' light of me and runnin' me ragged. Treatin' me like he treated his boots, only worse. At least I didn't have to fuck the son of a bitch. But you — you think you can have it just any old time you want it. You think you deserve it because I led you to this here mine — the Dutchman's mine — and now you're just feelin' like the cock o' the walk!"

225

The girl spat to one side, looked at Miller again, and wrinkled her other nostril.

Miller studied her, squinting against the bright sunlight up here at the top of a small, shelving mesa straight north of El Sombrero. "Hey, now . . . I was just funnin' you, girl. I was just feelin' good, and, you know . . . funnin'. No need to get a bur in your bonnet."

"I ain't wearin' a bonnet, you jackass."

"Hey, now, you listen here!" Miller said, feeling anger burn up through all the goodness and lightness he'd been feeling.

The girl reached behind her, filled her right hand with her pocket pistol. Miller had been moving toward her but now he stopped. His anger burned hotter, brighter.

"I was gonna wait till we got to Mexico, Pima," Jodi said, aiming the pistol at his belly. "I was gonna wait till we had the gold stashed somewhere secret, where we could fish it out whenever we needed more of it. It'd have been a whole lot easier to have help gettin' the gold across the border. But you won't make it. That wound done opened up on you. Opened up bad."

Miller glanced down at his side. She'd been right. He felt as though a sharp-toothed animal were gnawing away at the bullet hole. Blood stained his shirt. The stain was at least as large around as his open hand.

"You're losin' blood fast," Jodi said. "You'll just keep losin' it faster an' faster. And your slow dyin' would just slow me down. So I'm gonna end it right here, Pima."

The girl raised the pistol and clicked the hammer back. She smiled with one half of her mouth. "I'm gonna end our delightful partnership right here."

There was the *boing!* of a bowstring being released.

A soft whistling growing louder.

The thump of the arrow tearing into flesh and bone.

"Ughh!" the girl cried, lurching forward and triggering her pistol into the ground near her boots.

Dropping the gun, she twisted around and hooked an arm behind her back, which was suddenly bristling with a red-and-blue-fletched Chiricahua arrow sticking straight out from between her shoulder blades.

The afternoon before, after Hawk's and Saradee's own encounter with the Apaches, the rogue lawman managed to run down one of the Chiricahua's horses — a cream with cinnamon speckles across its rump and down its hips — and he and Saradee headed on down a twisting, turning arroyo to make camp a mile away from where the Chiricahuas lay moldering in the desert heat.

Hawk hadn't seen the old prospector since the man had wandered off in search of his burros. He figured the man had gone his own way, but when the purple evening shadows were stretching long and Hawk was perched on a rock at the lip of the arroyo, on the scout for more attackers, his Apache carbine resting across his thighs, he saw the lone figure moving toward him along the wash.

Two pack-laden burros flanked the bearded desert rat.

Saradee sat atop another rock on the wash's far side. Between her and Hawk, a low fire built from the near-smokeless branches of the catclaw shrub snapped and crackled, a pot of coffee gurgling as it warmed. She, too, watched as the man walked slowly toward them, his crunching foot thuds and the clomps of the burros rising gradually in the quiet desert gloaming.

"Company for dinner tonight," Saradee said in her wistful tone. "Hope the maid polished the silver."

As the stranger approached, he paused, blinking owlishly as he gazed at Hawk and

228

Saradee. He glanced down at the fire and then swung the burrows, which he led by a stout rope, toward the horseshoe in the wash in which Hawk and Saradee had tethered their horses, which were now eating mesquite beans.

A large, bloody jackrabbit hung down one side of one of the burros, the rope around the rabbit's neck tied to the pack frame.

The old man said softly, dully, "Meat for the fire."

He didn't say so, but Hawk knew it was an offering in return for Hawk and Saradee's intrusion on the Chiricahua's festivities, which doubtless had been about to include their seeing how loudly and for how long they could get the prospector to scream.

"That's funny," Hawk said, eyeing the bloody rabbit. "I didn't hear a shot."

As the desert rat began removing the pack frame from the back of his stockiest burro, Hawk saw the Apache war lance hanging from the frame, amid the bulging canvas panniers. The strap iron tip of the lance was still speckled with what appeared to be fresh blood.

Hawk gave a quiet chuff in recognition of the oldster's desert survival skills. Moving around out here as silently as possible was likely the reason he was still moving around at all.

When the prospector had finished unrigging and then carefully, thoroughly tending his burros, who snorted up the parched corn he'd mounded before them, he picked up an old Springfield rifle from among his gear. He walked shyly over to the fire, thumbing his hat back off his forehead and staring up at Saradee. The girl grinned at the old German, and climbed down off the boulder she'd been sitting on, one knee raised. She walked around the fire and stuck out her hand.

"I'm Saradee. Welcome to our fire!"

The old man looked at her hand. Apparently, he'd never shaken a female hand before. Haltingly, he lifted his own and gently squeezed Saradee's hand before running fingers through his grizzled beard and saying shyly, "You're right purty."

He'd said it so quietly that Hawk had barely heard him. The rogue lawman barely heard the oldster's low, sheepish chuckles as, steeling quick, frequent, admiring glances at the well-turned-out blonde before him, he dropped to his knees, slipped a knife from his belt sheath, and began deftly dressing the jack on a rock.

When the rabbit had finished roasting,

they all ate hungrily around the fire that they kept low, so the glow couldn't be seen for more than a few yards beyond it. The prospector didn't have much to say. Like most desert rats not accustomed to being around others, he was odd. He glanced around at Hawk and Saradee with a vague, speculative suspicion, as though he were wondering what they were doing out here.

He also cast Saradee several lusty looks, his glance dropping to the girl's swollen hickory shirt. Saradee pretended not to notice but only grinned over her plate or her raised coffee cup at him.

"I had one like you," the prospector said as he broke a rabbit bone and then loudly sucked out the marrow.

"You mean you had a woman," Saradee said with a dubious arch of her brows.

"Yep. I had one." The prospector rolled his dark eyes toward the darkness beyond the fire. "They killed her." He sighed, tossed his bones into the fire. "Killed her bloody, the devils."

That was the extent of his conversation for the evening except for one more sentence, spoken when they'd cleaned up their eating utensils and Hawk was about to situate himself for taking the first night watch.

The old prospector had just reclined

against the bed he'd made of several blankets and a burlap feed pouch. "No need to keep scout."

And then he tipped his hat brim down over his eyes.

Hawk glanced at Saradee, who shrugged a shoulder and then spread her own bedroll. Confident that the old-timer's senses were even keener than Hawk's own, and likely finely attuned to the smell of stalking Chiricahuas, Hawk rolled out an Indian blanket and drifted into a deep, dreamless sleep.

He awoke before dawn. It was the old-timer who'd awakened him. The man was outfitting his burros on the far side of the wash. When he had them rigged up, he simply walked away, leading the burros. His and the burros' footsteps dwindled gradually against the backdrop of a single, howling coyote.

Saradee was sitting up, leaning back on her elbows.

"What do you think about him?" she asked.

"I think I'm gonna follow him," Hawk said.

"How come?"

"Got a feelin' . . ."

Hawk flung his blanket aside, rose, and grabbed his rifle.

CHAPTER 19
IN THE DINOSAUR'S MOUTH

"I'll be damned," Hawk said the next day.

"What is it?"

On one knee atop a ragged-edged, red stone ridge, Hawk trained Saradee's spyglass through a notch overlooking a broad, red stone canyon with more red crags, like gothic church steeples, looming on the other side of it. Hawk and his blonde companion were at the heart of the Superstitions, among the towering peaks, plummeting canyons, and narrow, meandering washes littered with volcanic rubble.

This dramatic part of the range was a rocky waste composed of red rock striated like a giant turtle shell and liberally adorned with ancient petroglyphs. All that grew here were sparse bunches of Mormon tea, prickly pear, and ocotillo. Such ragged life had a tough fight, competing as it did with so much rock.

Mostly, the area was a beguilingly beautiful, three-dimensional statue of a dinosaur's mouth that seemed to have been carved from one massive chunk of volcanic ash and basalt and set down here in the heart of the Arizona desert. The cobalt blue of the sky arching over the awful formations gave it a mind-jarring depth.

"Don't see him," Hawk grunted, continuing to stare through the glass, sweeping the single sphere of magnified vision up and down the uneven floor of the canyon beyond and below him.

"We saw him turn into that canyon, lover. He's gotta be there, looking for his mine. If he really is the Dutchman, like you think he is."

"He is," Hawk growled, stung by her having called him "lover" again. Every time she used the moniker, it was like razor-edged claws raking the back of his neck.

He collapsed the spyglass and then began moving carefully down the steep, stone-carpeted slope toward where Saradee sat her palomino, holding the rope reins of Hawk's appropriated Apache mustang. His Apache carbine hung down Hawk's back by its leather lanyard, and his Apache bandanna ruffled in the hot breeze, the dry edge of which burned his eyes and made him forever thirsty. He was fortunate it was the monsoon season, and water was plentiful in the natural tanks among the rocks.

He paused now beside one such tank — little more than a shallow, egg-shaped dimple eroded out of the mosaic-like stone slope, in the shade of a square basalt boulder. He cupped the tepid water to his mouth, sucking it up and feeling the freshness roll down his throat. When he'd slaked his thirst, he removed his bandanna, soaked it, wrung it out only a little, and wrapped it around his head once more.

The wet cloth was instantly refreshing, cooling.

Hawk's thoughts were on the bearded stranger. Hawk figured the man, the "Dutchman" — who else could he be? — was heading for his secret mine, taking a roundabout route due to the comings and goings of the small bands of Apaches that roamed this stony wilderness, protecting their Thunder God from interlopers.

If so, the Dutchman might very well lead Hawk to Pima Miller and Jodi Zimmerman.

As long as the girl had actually been heading for the mine herself, of course. It was entirely likely she'd only been spewing hot air about knowing where the mine was located. Hawk didn't doubt she was more than a little soft in her thinker box. She might have only imagined she'd discovered the Dutchman's famously secret mine.

But following the so-called Dutchman had been Hawk's only hope of catching up to Miller, for it was impossible to track anyone through such rocks as those that comprised the Superstitions. Of course, Hawk could have let the man go in hopes of catching up to him later, in less forbidding territory.

But it was more than likely that Miller would head for Mexico after this, and Hawk might never get the chance to finally give him the bullet he was due. The bullet that he'd inadvertently given to the man's woman, Nan-tee, leaving their infant son an orphan.

Killing Miller wouldn't make up for Hawk's deadly mistake, of course. But it would make him sit a little easier, if such a thing were possible.

No, he wouldn't let Miller go. He'd try everything he could to run him down as fast as he possibly could. He didn't have anywhere special to be. If he died here, hunting Miller, so be it.

Men had died for worse causes than killing a killer like Miller. One who'd left his own boy behind . . .

Hawk continued down the slope. He tossed the spyglass up to Saradee. She tossed his rope rein down to him, and he had to leap, Apache-like, onto the rope saddle, which sported no stirrups. He reined the horse around — it was a fiery mount, and he had to keep it on a short leash lest it throw him — and rode along the bottom of the canyon they'd been following all morning.

The canyon slanted upward and dog-legged to the right. The horses' hooves clacked on the canyon floor's solid stone slab. The hot breeze wheezed among the towering peaks and ratcheted the branches of a near ocotillo.

Hawk turned the mustang around a mushroom-shaped scarp into the mouth of the canyon that he and Saradee had seen the Dutchman turn into about an hour ago. This was a narrow, winding cavity that appeared to climb gradually toward little but the blue sky far beyond.

They rode for an hour, the sun hammering down on them, and then suddenly Hawk's horse stopped and tossed its head and rippled its withers.

"Hold on," Hawk said, tightening his hold on the horse's rope rein, squeezing his knees against the mustang's sides. Getting pitched here onto solid rock could mean death or at least a broken bone or two.

In the distance, a gun popped. Saradee's palomino jerked, sidestepped. There was another pop and then another until it became obvious that several guns were being triggered farther up the trail, which appeared to grow steeper not far ahead. The gunfire continued — sporadic but angry, spanging shots — and then Hawk could hear men yelling, as well.

The sounds were growing louder.

From up trail, the trouble was moving toward him and Saradee.

Both Hawk and the girl leaped down from their horses, tied the reins to some tough, brown shrubs growing between boulders, and ran up the trail. They stopped at the brow of the next steep rise. From here Hawk could see the canyon they'd been following twist around to the right and climb more steeply before disappearing in chunks of red basalt capping a razor-back ridge.

Hawk swung the Apache carbine around to his front, and poked his finger through the trigger guard, his heart beating faster. He dropped to one knee, ran a hand across his mouth, and stared up to where the canyon trail climbed and disappeared in the crags.

He was thinking that the Dutchman had run into an Apache patrol.

"Hawk!"

He turned to his right. Saradee was standing and pointing toward where several dark, willowy figures clad in calico headbands were scrambling down from the giant, jutting rocks protruding straight up from the ridge. The Apaches were running down toward Hawk and Saradee.

Just then, one of the Apaches dropped to a knee, raised a carbine to his shoulder, and showed a flash of teeth in his brick-red face as he snapped off a shot, his rifle barking hollowly, the slug screeching off a boulder slightly upslope from Hawk and his blonde companion.

Hawk snapped up his own carbine and returned fire once, twice, three times, the rifle screeching and lurching in his hands.

"Free the horses!" he shouted, rising and snatching his mustang's reins from the shrub he'd tied them to. At the same time, Saradee did the same. They couldn't risk their horses being killed out here in this natural sarcophagus. Better to run them down later.

Neither mount needed encouragement. As the Apaches continued firing their repeaters while they ran down the slope, both mounts gave shrill whinnies and then scrambled around wildly and galloped back down the slick, rocky slope, their hooves slipping so that several times they both nearly fell.

Hawk ran up the slope toward the Apaches. He'd known from being in Apache country before, and encountering Apaches from several different bands, that there was no running from the warriors. They were like wildcats. You had to bring the battle to them, and you cut loose with as much ferocity as they did. It was your only chance.

Hawk just hoped that he and Saradee weren't so badly outnumbered that their efforts would be in vein.

Suddenly, Hawk wasn't so sorry to have Saradee at his side. She had no trouble, even facing Apaches, to bolt forward whooping and hollering, every few steps stopping, raising her own carbine, and triggering .44 rounds toward the little, savage men bolting toward her.

Hawk felt a grim smile shape itself on his lips as he ran around the left side of a cabin-sized boulder, hearing Saradee screeching and firing on the boulder's opposite side. The girl was too damned much like himself.

Gonna be a shame to kill her . . .

He paused in his own sprint toward the ridge to snap off another round. He watched one of the Apaches fold like a pocketknife and turn a forward somersault off the boulder he'd just fired from.

Hawk glanced to his right as Saradee triggered her own carbine. An Apache about thirty yards upslope from her gave a screech, dropped and rolled. He piled up about ten feet in front of the blonde, who gained her feet, strode purposefully toward the howling brave bleeding from the bullet wound in his bare chest, and calmly blew the top of his head off.

She glanced at Hawk, winked, and cast her gaze upslope as she ejected the spent shell casing and seated a fresh one in the chamber. Hawk moved forward, aiming his own carbine straight out from his right hip, sliding it from side to side. Two more figures ran leaping down from the ridge straight above him, and then he saw two more leaping down from above and left.

At the same time, the shooting on the other side of the ridge was growing louder, as though the separate shoot-out was moving toward him.

Rifles crackled above Hawk. He dropped behind a boulder as the bullets plunked into the rocks around him. He snaked his rifle over the top of the rock, aimed at a lean brave running low between rocks, making his gradual way toward Hawk's position.

Hawk fired, watched his bullet kick up

rock dust upslope from the brave continuing to work down toward him. At the same time, he spied movement in the upper-left periphery of his vision.

Hawk ejected the spent shell casing and looked toward where the canyon trail disappeared among the boulders capping the ridge, above and to his left. A man and two horses were running down from the ridge along the canyon trail. The man was running fast but stopping now and then to trigger lead back in the direction from which he was fleeing.

Crouched behind his covering rock, the rogue lawman began sliding fresh cartridges from the loops on his leather lanyard through the loading gate on his carbine. Two loud blasts sounded from upslope, not far away. The slugs hammered the opposite side of his covering boulder, blowing rock shards up and over his head.

He edged a peek over the rock to see the raisin-like face of a middle-aged Apache aiming an old Spencer repeater at him from the notch between two abutting boulders, twenty yards upslope from him. Hawk ducked as the rifle lapped flames toward him. The bullet screeched through the air where his head had been and puffed dust in the trail at the canyon bottom.

A rare apprehension raked the rogue lawman. During his peek over the top of the rock he was crouched behind, he'd seen more than merely the old Apache bearing down on him. He'd seen at least three more braves dropping down from the rocks capping the ridge. They seemed to be angling toward him and Saradee from the left, as if they were breaking off from the separate fight over that way.

His blonde partner must have gotten the same idea.

"Hey, Hawk!" Saradee called. She was belly down behind a large scarp to Hawk's right, sort of angled toward him, her carbine in her hands. He could see her bright, white smile through her delighted grin beneath the brim of her hat. "I think we might be about to powwow with old Geronimo — what do you think of that, lover?"

She laughed and fired her carbine.

CHAPTER 20
POWWOWING WITH GERONIMO

Another rifle blast caused Hawk's covering rock to quiver. Shards flew.

Gritting his teeth, Hawk lifted his head and rifle above the rock, planted a bead on the raisin-like forehead of the middle-aged Apache bearing down on him, and fired.

The Apache's head jerked back and then the man's arms and rifle came up as he flopped back and down and out of sight. He hadn't hit the ground before Hawk was up and running, triggering his carbine from his hip as he wove between boulders. One, two, three Apaches hit the dust and then one retaliating slug tore across the rogue lawman's left shoulder. The peripheral pain was an icy burn.

He shot the Apache who'd caused the burn but another appeared between two cabin-sized slabs of rock and sailed a slug over Hawk's left shoulder. He tried to return fire but his Winchester's hammer pinged on an empty chamber.

He ran another step then dove behind a wagon-sized boulder and immediately started reloading his carbine. Something moved to his hard left. He dropped the half-loaded Winchester, slid the Schofield from his cross-draw holster and raised the pistol as he clicked the hammer back.

Hawk stayed the pressure on the Schofield's trigger. He blinked. Pima Miller was hunkered down behind a boulder only a few yards up the slope from Hawk's position. The outlaw was hastily reloading Hawk's Henry, casting quick, sharp, shrewd glances toward the rogue lawman.

Hawk's heart thudded.

Rage welled in him. It was about to explode like a barrel of coal oil, when something moved on the boulder above Miller. Instinctively, Hawk shot the Apache bearing down on Miller. The warrior gave a shrieking cry. His own momentum drove him on over the boulder, dropping his rifle and clamping his hand across the bullet hole below his breastbone just before he turned a somersault and hit the rocky ground beside the outlaw Hawk was hunting.

Miller glanced at the dead Apache, and grinned. "Thanks, Hawk! 'Preciate that!"

Then he twisted around, aiming Hawk's

Henry repeater, and fired somewhere up-slope beyond Hawk's position. Hawk clicked the Schofield's hammer back but before he could aim again at his adversary, he saw another Apache running along the slope beyond the outlaw.

The brave was bearing down on Miller who just then saw him and triggered an errant round.

Hawk's Schofield barked twice. The Apache jerked as he ran, dropped to his knees, his bow and arrow clattering beside him, blood welling from the two holes in his chest, and collapsed facedown. He rolled on down the slope to pile up against a boulder thirty yards away from Miller.

Miller smiled. Hawk's heart continued to thud against his ribs as he tightened his grip on the Schofield, boring a hole through Miller with his eyes.

"Behind you!" the outlaw cried.

Hawk twisted around and triggered his Schofield. His bullet sailed wide of the Apache storming toward him, but two shots sounded from downslope. The Apache grunted and bounded upslope and then rolled back down past Hawk.

Hawk looked over the writhing Apache at Saradee. She was crouching behind a rock thirty yards away and on his right.

The Apache was trying to gain his feet while sliding a bowie knife from behind his deerskin sash. Hawk shot the brave through his right temple and then looked over the dead Indian toward Saradee, who, looking beyond Hawk, said, "I see you found one of your friends, lover!"

Hawk was only vaguely aware of clouds having moved over the sun as he turned back to Pima Miller, who was on his knees now and aiming Hawk's Henry repeater over the top of his rock. Miller was looking at Hawk over his right shoulder, grinning that faintly jeering grin of his.

"We're in this together, Hawk! You an' me now! Even your purty friend, if you trust her." The killer lifted his chin toward the ridge. "I left three saddlebags filled with gold over yonder. Couldn't get 'em off the mesa. Leastways, not with them redskins houndin' my heels. The girl's dead. Died hard!"

The Indians were still shooting but more sporadically. Saradee was returning fire with her carbine. Miller squeezed off a shot and then looked at Hawk again as he ejected the spent cartridge. It clattered onto the rocks and rolled as he slid another one into the Henry's breech.

"Hawk, for chrissakes — get your head

down!" Saradee admonished him.

The rogue lawman ignored her. He was staring grimly at Miller, not bothering to keep his head down any longer. He had killing on his mind. There was nothing else.

Only killing Pima Miller. That was why he was here.

Hawk rose stiffly from behind his cover. He did not look upslope. He was staring at Miller, who suddenly looked fearful. He laughed to try to cover it, but then his eyes grew dark, afraid.

"Hawk, fer chrissakes!" he shouted, glancing nervously upslope from where suddenly no more rifles barked, as though Hawk suddenly rising from behind his rock had befuddled the Indians to silence. "It's us against them, now, Hawk. We gotta put the past behind us. I left thousands of dollars in gold up yonder. Next mountain to the north! *Hundreds of thousands of dollars!*"

Behind Hawk, Saradee laughed. Hawk only vaguely heard her. He was on his feet now and he was moving toward Miller. He could feel the Apaches' eyes on him. He could feel their rifles trained on him.

He didn't care. Linda and Jubal were beckoning.

This was as good a day as any to join them. No one here deserved to live, anyway.

Not Miller. Not Saradee.

Not himself.

He was tired.

He just kept seeing that poor Indian woman he'd killed with a bullet meant for Miller. He kept seeing that little brown baby that Miller had left behind. He kept seeing in the far, misty background Linda and Jubal waving and smiling and beckoning him home.

A chill wind rose. Hawk heard it howling among the crags. The red rocks around him had turned gray as death.

"Hawk!" Miller cried. "You stop right there, goddamnit, or I'll shoot ya with your own gun!"

Hawk wasn't aware that he'd moved so swiftly until he saw his right, moccasin-clad foot lift. Then the Henry was rising up and over the boulder Miller was crouched behind. It turned in the air and then dropped out of sight. Hawk heard it clatter onto the rocks.

Behind Hawk, Saradee was laughing hysterically.

"Miller, do you really think Gideon Hawk gives a shit about *money*?" she cried.

Silence except for the moaning wind now hovered over the slope. That and Saradee's bizarre laughter that Hawk could barely hear.

Miller stared up at the rogue lawman standing over him, staring down at him. Miller's lower jaw hung. His narrow eyes were dark, terrified.

"Why, you're plum crazy," he rasped.

And then suddenly Miller was dragging his pistol out of its holster but before he could get it even half raised, Hawk smashed the butt of his carbine against the dead center of the man's forehead. The blow snapped Miller's head back against the rock with a crunching thud.

It stunned the killer, who sat staring dumbly at Hawk's belly.

"That there was for the woman," Hawk grunted.

He rammed the butt of the carbine against Miller's head again.

Miller grunted.

Hawk said, "That there's for the boy."

Again, he rammed the gun against the outlaw's bloody forehead.

"That was for the sawbones in Spotted Horse."

He raised the rifle once more, gritting his teeth and narrowing his eyes.

"This one's for me."

And then he drove the butt against the

killer's head one more time, harder than before. A resounding, crunching blow.

Miller's head bounced off the boulder. It jerked forward. The boulder behind him was red, speckled white with brain matter. Miller's shoulders followed his head over his knees, and then the killer rolled downslope three times before coming to rest on his back, his arms and legs akimbo.

His bashed-in forehead faced the sky. His lips were stretched back from his teeth in silent agony. His close-set, sightless eyes stared at nothing.

A horse nickered.

Hawk lifted his gaze from Miller. His grulla stood a ways downslope, beyond Miller. The girl's Morgan was there, as well, idly cropping the sparse brush growing around the base of a rock.

Hawk's grulla stared at its rider, head down, nose working. It twitched its ears and whickered with quiet urgency.

Hawk smiled.

Thunder rumbled.

He turned toward the upslope. Ten or so Indians had formed a semicircle around him, about twenty yards away. They crouched cautiously over their cocked rifles, all of which were aimed at Hawk's chest and belly.

"Sorry, Hawk," Saradee said behind him. She was no longer laughing. "I done capped my last shell. I'm fresh out. I reckon this is it, you crazy bastard."

Hawk looked at the braves. Most were young and clad in green, red, or gray calico headbands. They wore breechclouts and moccasins. Some wore deerskin leggings, the tops turned down.

They stared at Hawk quietly, mouths open, disbelief in their chocolate eyes. Their long, blue-black hair blew in the chill wind.

Cold raindrops began spitting down from the gray sky that was tearing on the highest crags.

Not all of the Chiricahuas facing Hawk were young. One was older, maybe late fifties, early sixties. Short and stocky, bandy-legged, streaks of silver in his long hair, he stood atop a boulder upslope from the others. His face was the nut-brown of old, worn leather, the skin drawn taught over high, knobby cheekbones. He wore a calico shirt and high-topped moccasins, a red sash around his lean waist.

A medicine pouch and a talisman of porcupine quills hung from his neck. His silver-black eyes were set deep in craggy sockets. He held a Spencer repeater down low by his side, the rifle's rear stock trimmed with brass rivets.

The wind swirled, carrying the older Chiricahua's distinct scent down toward Hawk. He smelled like the old, wild things of the desert.

The older Apache stared at Hawk. Hawk stared back at him. They stood silently regarding each other for nearly a minute.

And then Hawk turned his face a little to one side, quirked his lip corners with the respect due a formidable fellow warrior. And then he dropped his own carbine and held his arms out from his sides, palms raised slightly.

Opening himself to a life-ending hail of lead.

He waited.

The old warrior chief continued staring obliquely down at the rogue lawman.

Thunder crackled quietly at first — a long, ripping tear that grew louder and louder. When it finished echoing around the crags, the old man shouted something skyward, as though to his own Apache god.

And then all the young warriors turned and scrambled back up the slope. When they were out of sight, the old warrior dropped down off his boulder, glanced once more at Hawk, and then ambled in his lurching, crouching, bandy-legged gait up the slope. He held his carbine down low at his side, the lanyard swinging free.

The rocks at the top of the ridge seemed to swallow him up.

Thunder pealed.

Hawk lowered his arms. Rain lashed down at him. Still, he continued staring at where the old warrior had disappeared.

"Sorry, Hawk," Saradee said, coming up to stand beside him. They were both soaked, the rain hammering them.

Saradee patted the rogue lawman's chest. "Maybe some other time, lover. Come on," she said. "I'll buy ya a drink . . . somewhere warm. I know a place in Phoenix."

She slogged off down the rain-washed, rocky slope, thunder clapping, lightning dancing around her.

And still Gideon Hawk stared up the slope toward the misty crags. He squinted his eyes against the rain. He was looking for Linda and Jubal. He wanted to see them there, beckoning.

But they were gone.

Hawk dropped to his knees, sobbing.

The wind and rain lashed him.

Thunder was a giant war drum exploding in his head.

He didn't see the old Dutchman, Jacob Walzer, smiling down from his relatively sheltered hiding place among the crags not far from where Geronimo and his Chiricahuas had disappeared.

■ ■ ■ ■

Blood and Lust in Old Mexico

CHAPTER 1
RAINY NIGHT IN SONORA

The Rio Concho Kid sagged back in his rickety chair and listened to the soft desert rain drum on the cantina's tin roof while a lone coyote howled mournfully in the Forgotten Mountains to the south.

The Kid was pleasantly drunk on *bacanora,* a favorite drink of the border country. He smiled sweetly as he reflected on happier times, hopeful times when he and his reputation were still young and, if not innocent, at least naive.

Mercifully, just when his thoughts began to sour, touching as they did on the smiling visage of a fresh young Apache girl named Elina, who was so long dead that he could just barely remember the texture of her hair but no longer recall the timbre of her voice, hooves hammered the muddy trail outside the remote cantina's batwing doors.

For an instant, a single owl's cry, like a fleeting call of caution, drowned that of the coyote.

Over the doors, out in the dark, rainy night, a large shadow moved. The smell of wet horse and wet leather, as well as the faint fragrance of cherry blossoms, wafted in on the chill damp air.

Leather squawked and a horse chomped its bridle bit.

Boots thumped on the narrow wooden stoop, and then a shadow appeared and became a young, red-haired woman as she pushed through the batwings and stopped, letting the louver doors clatter back into place behind her. Hunted brown eyes quickly scanned the long, dark, earthen-floored cantina, finding its only customer, the Kid, lounging against the wall opposite the bar consisting of cottonwood planks laid across beer kegs.

The barman, Paco Alejandro Dominguez, was passed out in his chair behind the clay *bacanora* bowl, snoring softly, his thick gray hair tumbling down over his wizened, sun-blackened face. His leathery, hawk nose poked through the hair, nostrils expanding and contracting as he snored.

The girl glanced behind her, nervous as a doe that had just dropped a fawn, and then strode forward to the Kid's table.

She was a well-set-up girl, twenty at the

oldest, her thick, wavy, rust-red hair falling down over her shoulders and onto her plaid wool shirt that she wore open to the top of her cleavage. Between her breasts, a small, silver crucifix winked in the salmon light of the mesquite fire crackling near the bar's far end and in front of which a kitten snoozed in a straw basket.

The girl wore black leather slacks held snug to her comely hips by a leather belt trimmed with hammered silver, five-pointed stars. Black boots with silver tips rose to her shapely calves. There were no spurs. This was a girl who could ride — she had the hips and the legs for it — but who had a soft spot for horses.

Her hair was damp, as was her shirt, which clung to her full bosom, and her eyes were just wild enough to make the Kid's trigger finger ache.

"Buy a girl a drink?" she said quickly in a thick Spanish accent.

The Kid looked her over one more time, from the tips of her boots up past her breasts pushing out from behind the damp wool shirt, to her eyes that flicked back and forth across him with a faint desperation. The Kid smiled, shook his head. His dark eyes looked away from the young girl, no more than a child.

She slammed her fist on the table. *"Bas-tardo!"*

"I ain't gonna contest it," the Kid said mildly and casually lifted his gourd cup to sip his *bacanora.*

She lifted her mouth corners, leaned forward against the table, giving him a better look down her shirt, and said in a smoky, sexy rasp: "I could make you a very happy *hombre* tonight, *amigo.*"

The Kid looked at her well-filled shirt. A few years ago, when he was as green as a willow sapling, such a sight would have grabbed him by the throat and not let go for several hours. "And a dead one. Oh, true, there's worse things than dyin', but I'm enjoyin' this evenin' here with the rain and my drink and the prospect of a long sleep in a deep mound of straw out in the stable with my mare, Antonia. Run along, *chiquita.* Spread your happiness to someone who needs it more than I do tonight."

The Kid reached into the breast pocket of his buckskin shirt for his tobacco makings, but stopped suddenly and pricked his ears. Hooves drummed in the distance, beneath the patter of the rain on the tin roof and the cracking and popping of the pinyon fire in the mud-brick hearth.

The girl wheeled toward the batwings with a gasp.

The hoof thuds grew quickly louder. The girl's horse whinnied. One of the newcomers' horses whinnied a response. Over the batwings, large shadows moved, and then boots thudded on the porch and a big man in a wagon-wheel sombrero pushed through the batwings.

Two men flanked him, turning their heads this way and that to see around him, into the cantina.

"No, Chacin," the girl said in a brittle voice, backing away from the door, brushing the tips of her fingers across the Kid's table. "I won't . . . I won't go with you. I'd rather *die!*"

All this had been in Spanish, but the Kid, who'd been born Johnny Navarro in the Chisos Mountains of southern Texas, near the Rio Grande, though he'd acquired his nickname while riding the long coulees along the Rio Concho, knew the rough and twisted border tongue as well as he knew English.

The big man, dressed in the flashy gear of the Mexican *vaquero,* complete with a billowy green silk neckerchief, moved heavily into the room, bunching his thick, mustache-mantled lips in fury. His chocolate eyes fired golden javelins of rage as water dripped from the brim of his black-felt wagon-wheel sombrero.

"*Chiquita,* my orders are to bring you back to the General! You're lucky you didn't kill him — at least not yet!"

Suddenly, moving with more agility than the Kid would have thought possible in a man so ungainly, he swiped one of his big paws at the girl and caught her shirt just as she'd turned to run. The shirt tore with a shrill ripping sound, buttons popping, exposing a good portion of her pale left breast behind her partially torn chamise.

She screamed, *"No!"*

The big man reached for the silver-plated Colt Navy conversion pistol holstered high on his right hip.

"Oh, now, dangit," the Kid said with an air of great despondency, rising heavily from his table and brushing his right hand across the Smith & Wesson Model 3 Schofield revolver holstered high and for the cross draw on his left, denim-clad hip, "that ain't no way to treat a lady, an' you *know* it!"

CHAPTER 2
THE RIO CONCHO KID RIDES

The big Mexican must not have heard the Kid's indictment, for he slid his long-barreled Colt from its holster and was thumbing the hammer back when the Kid's own revolver roared like close thunder, causing the earthen floor to jump and the ceiling to buffet.

"Ah, Mariett-ahhhh!" the barman cried, lurching straight up out of his chair, still half asleep.

Dust sifted from between the herringbone pattern of cottonwood and mesquite branches to the floor.

The big Mexican, Chacin, squealed pig-like and fell back against a table, clutching the hole in the dead center of his chest. The hole was pumping blood like a geysering spring. He got his boots beneath him, held himself upright though listing badly to his left, regarding the Kid with shock and fury blazing like lamps in his dark eyes.

The girl backed away from him, covering her mouth with both her gloved hands. Chacin squeezed his eyes closed and fell with a heavy thump to the earthen floor, and lay with one leg quivering as he finished dying.

"Dios!" exclaimed the barman, Paco Alejandro Dominguez, crossing himself as he looked over the bar to the big man on the floor.

The Kid clicked his Schofield's hammer back and aimed at the two men who'd entered with Chacin. They both stood in crouches, hands on their holstered weapons, staring at the Kid apprehensively. One of them was slowly inching his walnut-gripped Remington up out of its black-leather holster thonged low on his right thigh. His hand was shaking.

He stared at the Kid's gun. Smoke slithered like a little gray worm from the round, dark maw.

Chacin's men looked at each other, wide-eyed. Then, keeping their hands on their holstered weapons but keeping the weapons in their holsters, they shuffled backward through the batwings to fade away in the dark, wet night.

"Kid!" said Dominguez, his rheumy eyes round with fear. He jutted a gnarled finger at the big, dead Mexican on the floor. In

Spanish, he said, "That is Chacin Velasco, General Constantin San Gabriel's right-hand man!"

The Kid turned to the girl who was still staring down at the dead man, both hands closed over her mouth. She turned to him slowly, lowering her hands. She said in a voice the Kid could barely hear above the pattering rain, "*Muchas gracias, senor.* It is unfortunate that I cannot give you my life, which I owe you for saving, because I am afraid I have just cost you yours."

Boots thumped on the porch. The Kid turned toward the front of the cantina once again, just as Chacin's two men, apparently realizing that they themselves were dead men unless they killed the man who'd killed Chacin, came bursting through the batwings like Brahma bulls through a loading chute.

Their gloved hands were filled with iron.

The Kid's Schofield thundered twice, sending both men bounding back through the doors, triggering their pistols into the cantina floor, and into the cool, wet night. They dropped with heavy smacking thuds, causing the horses to whinny and nicker and pull against their reins.

The Kid turned to the girl who stood smiling at him. The smile irritated him nearly as much as his having to kill three men just now when he was merely wanting to drink himself drunk and then to stagger out to Dominguez's stable and to sleep long and hard, old Antonia's somnolent breaths lulling him into peaceful dreams.

"What the hell is this about, *senorita*?"

She still had that nettling smile on her face. Her eyes were dreamy. "It's about love," she said. "What else is there?"

The Kid scratched the back of his head with his gun barrel. He was beginning to think she was soft in her thinker box. "Huh?"

"Love is a powerful thing. There will be more men where these men came from," she said, sobering and glancing at Chacin who lay still now in death. "I apologize, but it is true. If you help me to safety, you will be well rewarded."

Her eyes were smoky, insinuating, vaguely desperate, and she thrust her shoulders back slightly, impulsively, like a girl who knew exactly how desirable she was and used it to her best advantage.

The Kid looked at Dominguez. The old barkeep arched a brow at him.

"Get your horse," the Kid told the girl, breaking the "top-break" Schofield open to reload. "I'll fetch mine from the barn and meet you on the trail."

When he'd replaced the revolver's spent cartridges, he dropped it into its holster, snapped the keeper thong over the hammer, and walked toward the cantina's back door, casting incredulous glances at the beautiful girl behind him. He went out into the misty darkness laced with the smell of pinyon smoke and wet sage. He went into the adobe stable flanking the cantina — it was little more than an ancient, brush-roofed ruin — and found old Antonia snoring softly in her stable by a pile of aromatic hay.

A moody sorrel with gray spots sprayed across her hindquarters and a white star between her copper eyes, Antonia blew and stomped, cranky about being saddled so late, and in this weather, to boot! And the Kid said, "Know just how you feel, girl."

When he'd stuffed his old-model Winchester down into his elk hide saddleboot trimmed with Chiricahua beads, he mounted up and rode out, Antonia's hooves clomping dully on the wet ground. The girl sat her horse, a rangy Appaloosa, near some rocks and brush along the trail. The Kid saw her outline against the stars that were trying to break through the thin clouds that rolled across the sky like ink-stained tufts of gauze.

"Come on." He said it quietly, but the

moody night was so strangely silent that it sounded like a yell. "I know a place."

CHAPTER 3
LA PISTOLA SAYS IT BEST

A long, keening wail rose on the night's damp wind, ensconcing all of *Hacienda del la General Constantin San Gabriel* in wretched torment and poignant misery.

Around the *hacienda*'s walled grounds, the peons prayed in their tiny, thatch-roofed hovels while babies cried, dogs howled, goats brayed, and pinyon logs snapped in fieldstone hearths, the gray smoke ribboning like halfhearted prayers up sooty chimneys.

Inside the sprawling, cavern-like, tile-roofed adobe casa, the General himself lay moaning in blood-soaked sheets. He groaned as he chomped down on a swatch of leather cut from a boot as his gray-bearded, one-eyed attendant, Juan Mendoza, stitched the nasty knife wound in his side.

Kneeling in a dark corner near a crackling stove, *Padre* Vicente, cloaked in ragged

271

shadows, muttered over his prayer beads while a fat black cat washed its face on a window ledge beside him.

"That bitch! That bitch!" the General moaned. "I demand her beautiful, conniving head on a platter!"

The priest's muttering grew louder as he clutched his silver crucifix in both hands before him, occasionally pressing his lips to it.

"Si, si," said Juan Mendoza, pinching up the skin around the ragged, bloody wound. "Chacin will bring her kicking and screaming, General. She will get her comeuppance for what she did to you. Imagine such an insult . . . on your wedding night, no less!"

Mendoza squinted his lone eye, poked the fire-blackened point of his needle through the pinched skin, and drew the catgut taut.

The General threw his bearded head back on his pillow and bellowed at the herringbone rafters.

"The worst of it is," he cried, "I *loved* that red-haired bitch!"

When Mendoza had finished stitching the wound and was dabbing at it with arnica, hoof thuds rose beyond the window. Horses splashed through puddles and blew and shook their bridle bits.

"Chacin!" the General hissed, lifting his

head from the pillow and staring out the arched window. His eyes glowed with emotion as he stared into the night. He rose still higher and yelled in his weak, pain-pinched voice, "Chacin — report to me! Did you bring her?"

Outside, there was only the clomping and snorting of the horses beyond the wall of the General's wet garden.

"Chacin!"

General San Gabriel flung his covers away and dropped his pale feet to the cold flagstone floor.

"General!" admonished Juan Mendoza, placing a hand on the General's shoulder. "You must rest!"

The General brushed the man's hand away and heaved himself up off the bed, gritting his teeth against the searing pain in his side, where that bitch stuck the knife in just when he'd disrobed her fine body and was going to reward her with his own . . .

He stood, his broad torso bare, and grabbed his fleece-lined, red velvet robe off a chair back. The General was a tall, regal man with an impeccably trimmed mustache and goatee, hawk nose, and close-set, flinty eyes — the hard, shrewd eyes of a veteran of the bloody Mexican-American War and many, even bloodier battles against the hated Apache and Yaqui Indios.

For all of his sixty-two years, the General's coal-black hair and beard owned not a single strand of gray. His body was straight and, in spite of a slight paunch, as hard and sinewy-strong as that of an old warhorse.

With Mendoza and *Padre* Vicente hovering nervously around him, voicing their objections, the General drew the robe around his lean hips, and stepped into a pair of wool-lined doeskin sandals. He grabbed a Navy Colt conversion .36 off a low table beside his favorite, brocaded chair, quickly checked the loads, and dropped the brass-framed piece into a deep pocket of his robe.

He walked, cursing under his breath, through an arched door that gave access to his garden that was impeccably cultivated by the peons who'd come with the land he'd been granted by the government in Mexico — thirty-thousand acres of prime grazing land as payment for his near-lifelong service in the Mexican army.

His slippers clacked and scuffed against the flags as, holding one hand to the freshly stitched wound, he shuffled across the dripping garden and through an opening in the six-foot-high adobe wall into the soggy, muddy yard bordered by the *hacienda*'s several barns, the bunkhouse, and many pole corrals.

Lights from the peasants' shacks shone down the southern hill in the wooly darkness. A fine mist continued to fall, though several stars winked dully through the clouds.

Several riders sat their horses in front of the bunkhouse on the far side of the broad dirt yard from the General — part of the posse he'd sent after his bride. The riders were speaking in conspiratorial tones to four other *vaqueros* who stood smoking on the bunkhouse's brush-roofed gallery, the bunkhouse door open behind them and showing the flickering orange light of a fire.

Breeze-brushed, rain-beaded lanterns hanging beneath the gallery roof tilted shadows to and fro.

"Chacin!" the General bellowed, mindless of a pecan branch dribbling cold raindrops on his head and down his back. Mendoza and *Padre* Vicente stood in the opening in the wall behind him, cowering against the rain and hissing their disapproval of their *patrón*'s impetuousness.

The three riders whipped their sombrero-mantled heads toward the General. They glanced at each other dubiously and then, with a reluctant air, galloped over and stopped their horses in the hock-high mud before the *patrón*. Chacin Velasco was not among them.

Frowning, the General looked around. "Where is Chacin? Where is the girl? Where is my *wife*?"

"General, Lieutenant Velasco is dead!" intoned the *vaquero* known as Rubio something-or-other, his eyes concealed by the broad brim of his flat-crowned straw sombrero. "Him and two others were gunned down by a man as fast as God's angry fist from heaven!"

As if to punctuate the man's testimony, his horse whinnied and tried to buck, but the rider kept the wild-eyed barb on a tight rein.

General San Gabriel glowered at the man, his pain-addled brain slow to comprehend the information. Lieutenant Chacin Velasco, his most loyal officer . . . *dead*? It couldn't be. Chacin was not only proficient and quick with a gun, but he'd been the fiercest fighter the General had ever known. And he'd known a few!

Chacin had killed more Apaches than even the General himself!

"Nonsense," the General said though the shocked, apprehensive stares of the men before him tempered his resolve. "You must be mistaken. Who could kill Chacin? Surely not that little bitch who stabbed me when my defenses were down!"

Rubio and the man sitting the horse next to him both turned to the third rider, who said, "The Rio Concho Kid!"

"Who?"

The third rider repeated himself. And then in a few hastily spewed sentences, he filled his boss in on the rest of what had happened at Dominguez's cantina barely two hours ago. He and his two partners had ridden up to the cantina, where they were to rendezvous with Chacin, only to find Chacin and the two other *vaqueros* dead as tombstones.

Paco Alejandro Dominguez had informed them about who had done the killing only as an admonishment to let the man go. To go after such a man they'd need an army!

General San Gabriel stared up at the riders before him, silently fuming. "And you three listened to that old reprobate and did *nothing* but turn tail and *run*?"

"*Jefe*, you may not have heard of the Rio Concho Kid." The stocky man sitting in the middle of the small group shook his head slowly, darkly. "He is very deadly. He was just back from the War Between the States when he killed thirteen soldiers — *American soldiers!* — and desecrated their bodies in

277

the most horrible way imaginable. Very deadly, boss. The Rio Concho Kid. It is said that wherever he rides a demon follows in the form of a ghost-faced owl. This winged demon looks after the Kid."

"An *owl?*"

"*Si, si!* The Apache bird of grace and deliverance. You see, the Kid avenged the murders of his Apache brothers and sisters — he is half Apache himself though he more resembles his Anglo father — and, once they were avenged, the spirits of the dead sent the owl to follow and protect him until the Kid, too, enters the world of the spirits."

"The Rio Concho Kid," said the General, eyes sharp with fury. "Owls! Spirits! *Apaches!* Let me tell you what I think of you three, riding off and leaving Chacin's body to molder in that fetid cantina . . . *unavenged!*"

"No, General!" Rubio shouted as the old warrior pulled the Colt Navy out of his robe pocket and raised it, clicking the hammer back.

Rubio raised both his hands in front of his face a half second before the General's roaring Colt blew a hole through Rubio's right hand and into his right cheek, just beneath his eye.

Pow! Pow!

The other two riders flew off the backs of their horses to hit the ground with wet thuds. All three horses wheeled, whinnying shrilly, and ran off across the yard, buck-kicking wildly.

The General walked over to the stocky *vaquero* who was still writhing and groaning. "But why waste words when *la pistola* says it best?"

He aimed the smoking Colt down at a slant and triggered a finishing round into the *vaquero*'s broad forehead.

Behind the General, Mendoza stood hang-jawed in shock.

Padre Vicente sobbed, clutching his crucifix to his breast and staring toward the stars as though praying that God had not witnessed this atrocity.

Presently, hooves thudded.

The General turned his attention from the dead men sprawled before him toward another rider, this one with his face bizarrely masked in white, riding into the yard from the north.

CHAPTER 4
SATAN RIDES TO US THIS EVENING, AMIGOS!

The Rio Concho Kid brought his mare to a halt beside a jutting escarpment near the brow of a night-capped ridge. Leaning forward in his saddle, the Kid looked up at the top of the hill where an old Spanish mission church hulked, pale in the rain-scoured starlight.

An orange light flashed in the church's bell tower, over the black square of the broad open doorway. The Kid jerked his head back as the bullet hammered the front of the escarpment, inches from his face, the ricochet's shriek nearly drowning the rifle's flat report.

Behind the Kid, the girl gasped.

The Kid raised his own rifle and sent three rounds screeching toward the bell tower and the shadow crouching inside. The rifle in the bell tower flashed again, but this time the orange flame lapped toward the ground.

As the Kid pulled his rifle down while

pumping a fresh round into the chamber, he watched as the shadow in the bell tower slumped. The bushwhacker screamed a Spanish epithet, and then he fell forward out of the bell tower, his black silhouette turning a somersault against the cream tan of the adobe church.

There was a resounding thud and a splash as he struck a mud puddle. The lookout's rifle clattered to the muddy ground beside him.

Harsh voices rose from inside the church as did the metallic rasps of five or six rifles being cocked.

The Kid leaned forward in his saddle once more, clamping his rifle under one arm, raising both hands to his mouth, and shouting in Spanish, "Flee, you dogs. The Rio Concho Kid's come calling. He aims to take up residence here this evening, and he's not in the mood for company!"

A man's girlish shriek echoed inside the church. Boots clomped. Spurs rang.

A man shouted, *"Satanas cabalgo con nosotros esta noche, amigos!"*

A shrill Spanish curse.

More boot clomping and spur ringing. A few minutes later, while the Kid waited back behind the escarpment with the girl, hoof thuds rose from behind the church. They dwindled away to silence.

"All right," the Kid said, touching spurs to old Antonia's flanks and riding out from behind the scarp and onto the ridge.

The man he'd shot lay sprawled a few feet from the front of the block-like adobe church squaring its shoulders against the starry sky from which the storm clouds had disappeared. The damp air was cool and fresh, smelling like wild rose and cactus blossoms and brimstone.

"You sure know how to clear out a place." The girl stopped her horse suddenly. The Kid halted his own mount, turned toward her.

It was hard to see her face in the darkness, but he thought she was appraising him dubiously. Her long, red hair fluttered in a vagrant breeze.

"The Rio Concho Kid . . . ," she whispered.

Just then something gray flickered off to her left. She gasped as she turned her head and saw a ghost-faced owl wing past her. Its eyes glowed like umber coals in the darkness. The small, dove-gray bird gave its raucous, unsettling cry, which echoed harshly off the front of the church, before lighting on the front ledge of the bell tower and lifting a wing to preen.

The girl shuddered as she stared up at the sinister creature. "They say you're protected by Apache devils," the girl muttered. Her voice was thin, rife with caution.

"Guided, more like," the Kid said. "Not even an owl can protect me from some of the trouble I manage to court."

He swung down from his saddle and began leading Antonia to the front door. "Come on, if you've a mind. I told you I knew a place to shelter for the night, and this is it. If you don't like it . . . or the company . . . you're free to drift."

The Kid led Antonia into the church, pleased to see that the desperadoes had left a crackling fire near the front of the church, where an altar had once stood though it had long-since crumbled to jutting shards. What looked like a rabbit was spitted over the low flames.

The Kid had nearly finished unsaddling Antonia before slow clomps sounded, and he turned to see the girl leading her impressive Appaloosa through the large open doorway.

CHAPTER 5
TOMASINA DE LA CRUZ

The Kid walked back into the church after a thorough scout of the ridge, after both horses had been unsaddled and he'd made the girl comfortable by the fire. The blaze's warmth was welcome on such a damp and chilly evening.

She sat beside the fire, knees raised, a blanket over her shoulders. She was leaning forward and clutching the toes of her low-heeled, silver-tipped black boots. On the soles of each a red turtle had been stitched in red.

Her eyes were chocolate brown sprayed with flecks the same color as her hair, which, threaded with faint crimson highlights, hung straight down across her shoulders.

The Kid stopped before her, his rifle on his shoulder, and thumbed his brown Stetson back off his forehead. She looked up at him coyly, bouncing back and forth nervously on her rump while clutching her boot toes — an alluringly girlish gesture, thought the Kid.

But then everything about her — the smoothness of her skin, the fullness of her lips, the depth of her gaze, the sunset red of her hair — was strangely, almost uncomfortably alluring. Even her brandy-like smell, which he'd noticed on the trail, was intoxicating.

She glanced at a tin plate on which lay the lightly charred rabbit that the desperadoes had been roasting over the fire. Only a quarter of the carcass was missing. A cup of black coffee sat next to it, smoking.

"I left most of it for you, *senor,*" she said softly.

The Kid leaned his rifle against the wall and sat down near his saddle. He doffed his hat and gloves, scrubbed his hands through his close-cropped, coal-black hair, brushed a buckskin-clad sleeve across his broad, weathered forehead, and then set the plate on his knee.

He tore the rabbit in two, and glanced at the girl, who watched him steadily, expectantly, as though waiting for him to break out in song.

"The Rio Concho Kid," she said, making him uncomfortable again with her close, dubious scrutiny. "I did not know when I walked into *Senor* Dominguez's cantina that I would find such a man as you there."

"Just my luck." The Kid pushed a chunk of the rabbit into his mouth.

"I should have known that only the Rio Concho Kid could have killed Chacin Velasco so swiftly, without flinching."

She seemed to wait for the Kid's response, which did not come.

"How many men have you . . . ?" She let her voice trail off, her eyes brightening with trepidation, realizing that she might have crossed a dangerous boundary. "If you don't mind me asking, *senor.*"

"Enough that I can clear a church of the devil's hounds right fast," the Kid said, taking another bite of the rabbit. "You gonna tell me who you are and who you're runnin' from and why, or you intend on keepin' it under your hat?"

He continued to eat, and when the girl said nothing, he glanced at her. She was staring up into the darkness beyond the fire's umber, cinder-stitched glow. "The owl?" she said.

"Ah, don't mind him," said the Kid. "He comes, he goes. Tumbleweed, that one. Sorta like me an' ole Antonia. But, unlike me, he's somehow managed to keep a price

286

off his head. Now, if you don't mind explainin' why I'm not still pleasantly drunk and half asleep at Dominguez's place, and who I should be watchin' out for . . ."

"I am Tomasina De La Cruz," she said in her quiet, mysterious voice that was as captivating as the rest of her. "And I am on the run, as you say, from General Constantin San Gabriel."

The Kid choked on a bite of rabbit, and scowled across at her. "How in the hell — if you'll pardon my privy talk, *senorita* — did you manage to lock horns with *that* fork-tailed Apache-killer?"

Tomasina De La Cruz jerked a look at him, her eyes feisty. "I did not want to lock horns with him! I did not want to lock anything with him!" A chinking appeared in her armor as her voice trembled, and a shiny veil dropped down over her eyes. "It was my father who did. He wanted me to marry that dirty old man!"

"Why?"

She turned away from the Kid once more and raised her knees higher, wrapping her arms around them, as though for protection against some unseen beast in the darkness. "It was the arrangement. You see, my father owns a *hacienda* on the other side of a mountain pass from the General, who came

287

to the country of the Rio San Gezo only a few years ago. Having been in the military most of his life, he never married."

"And then he met you." The Kid knew how the General must have felt. The girl had a definite pull. The Kid felt it himself. A pull like only one other he'd ever felt.

"*Si,* he met me when my father invited him to *La Colina de Rosa,* on the opposite side of the Forgotten Mountains from the General's *hacienda.* He told me later he fell in love with me the first time he laid eyes on me." Tomasina shivered with revulsion.

"I take it the feeling wasn't shared." The Kid had been rolling a quirley with chopped Mexican tobacco and brown wheat paper. Now he reached for a brand in the fire, touched it to the quirley, sucked the peppery smoke deep into his lungs, and blew it out through his nostrils.

"No," she said, shaking her head slowly. "No, no . . ."

"And the General is not a man to take no for an answer."

"*Si.*"

She nodded gravely and then turned to the Kid again. "*La Colina de Rosa* has fallen on hard times. Our side of the mountains is in a drought. For the past three years, all the clouds pass over us and continue on over the mountains to drop their snow and rain on the General's *hacienda.* His creeks run deep with water, his grass grows stirrup-high. His cattle are fat and happy!"

Tomasina spat this last out like a bone as she kept her angry, wet gaze on the Kid. "My father and mother thought it best I marry the General, who could better provide for me. No one cared that I loved another!"

This last she fairly screamed. The scream rocketed around inside the church for too long, and the Kid winced and cast his gaze toward the open doorway, worried someone might have heard.

"*Senorita,* I know you're upset, but —"

She cut him off with "The marriage was arranged despite my protestations, *senor.*"

"Despite the fact you were in love with another."

"*Si* — Ernesto Alabando." She whispered the name, stretching her mouth to show all her small, pretty white teeth in an adoring smile. Slowly, her jaws drew taut, and she pressed her lips together until they formed a knife slash across the bottom half of her face.

Again, she turned her blazing eyes on the Kid.

"I tried to run away to Ernesto. The

General, however, is a jealous man, and a suspicious one, as well. He had ordered a man, a gun-toting leper — a bounty hunter — to keep a watchful on *La Colina de Rosa* . . . and me. When the leper foiled my attempt at escape, the General demanded we be married straightaway. After the ceremony at *La Colina,* he took me to his *rancho.* That night, after a grand but quiet meal — just the two of us and his servants — he ushered me off to his sleeping quarters, and disrobed me."

Tomasina De La Cruz clutched herself and shuddered as though deeply chilled.

"The thought of lying with this wheezing, warty, lusty old dog who had made me so unhappy, so lonely for Ernesto, *my one true love* — he so incensed me, you see, that before I knew what I was doing, I had grabbed one of the General's own fancy stilettos and stuck it in his guts!"

She cried for some time into her hands, her shoulders jerking, burnished copper hair falling down over her raised knees to hide her face.

"Pardon me, *senorita,*" the Kid said after what he thought was a discreet length of silence. "But . . . did you say *the Leper?*"

Chapter 6
A Plea and an Offer

Tomasina De La Cruz lifted her head, sniffed, brush tears from her cheeks, and nodded. *"Si. El Leproso."* She turned to him. "You know this man — this hideous creature?"

The Kid tossed his quirley stub into the fire. "Yeah. I know him."

The image of the man's misshapen face cloaked by a flour sack with the eyes and mouth cut out, caused icy fingers of dread to walk up and down his spine.

The girl crawled over to the Kid, knelt beside him, and placed both her hands on his right forearm. Her eyes were large as saucers, rife with beseeching. "Then you know what an awful man he is. A beast."

"A beast, all right," the Kid said, nodding, looking down at the girl's slender hands on his arm. "And damn handy with that shotgun of his." It was a sawed-off, double-barreled coach gun that the Leper, a Mexican bounty hunter, kept loaded with rock salt, because most of the higher-paying bounties were for men brought in with their ghosts intact.

The salt would make a mess of a man, but, if delivered to the right areas, it rarely killed, although its victims often wished they were dead.

"Por favor, senor," the girl said, squeezing his arm. "Will you help me? It is most likely that the General will send *El Leproso* for me, as he did once before."

"Help you do what, *senorita*? Help you *get where*?"

"To San Gezo. A two-day ride, only."

"What's in San Gezo?"

"Ernesto," she whispered, stretching her lips back away from her small, white teeth again. "My life's one true love. He will take me away to somewhere the General and *El Leproso* will never find us!"

The Kid looked down at her hands again. They burned into him, evoked a passion he'd rarely felt in his twenty-eight years. He lifted his gaze to her eyes. They were like a deer's eyes, wide with earnest pleading and boundless love, gazing up at him from beneath her brows.

Her rich, red lips were parted. Behind her

shirt, her breasts rose and fell slowly, heavily.

Ernesto was one lucky boy!

The Kid tore his arm from her grip, and turned away, repelled by his own passion evoked by this girl's love for her beau. Of course the General had tumbled for this girl. What man wouldn't?

Lucky Ernesto!

The Kid stared at the church wall left of the fire. It danced and pulsated with reflected firelight. But it was the Kid's own shameful lust he saw there in that crenellated, flame-lit wall.

This girl was a succubus. She had him in her snare.

But she loved another.

He jerked with a start when he felt her arms wrap around him from behind. He watched one arm snake across the other one, over his belly. She pressed her body against his back. It was warm, supple, yielding. He could feel her breasts mash into him.

They, too, were warm, compliant.

Frowning, he turned, placed his hands on her naked shoulders. Her head came up with the rich mass of copper hair. Her eyes bored into his. He lowered his own gaze, and a hot shaft of desire was plunged into his loins.

She'd taken off her shirt. She sat before him with her lovely, pale breasts bared to him, the pink nipples like tender rosebuds.

"I told you back in the cantina, Kid," she said softly, in that gut-wrenchingly sexy voice of hers, the tip of her pink tongue flicking at her lips as she spoke, "that if you helped me I would make you a very happy man. Well, maybe not happy. I know what happened to you, Kid. Everyone has heard about . . . your family . . . your woman . . . the soldiers. All the death, all the killing. The bounty on your head back north of the border. But at least let me reward you for your efforts tonight, as promised."

As he stared at her, rapt, she smiled gently and placed her hands on his. She lifted his hands, cupped them to her breasts.

She whispered very softly, "I have never lain with another. Not even Ernesto. Not yet. I guess that was partly my appeal for the General."

The Kid's tongue lay heavy in his mouth. "And . . . you would . . . lay . . . ?"

She smiled that surreal smile of hers. "You are a good man. Ernesto wouldn't mind. I will by lying with him soon."

Her soft, smooth skin fairly burned in the Kid's palms. The pink nipples raked him gently. He'd just started to roll his thumbs across the tender buds when the owl's ear-rattling shriek rose, echoing like large stones rattling around in a barrel plunging down a steep, rocky hill.

The Kid looked past the girl toward a rear door, and shouted, "Tomasina, *down!*"

He shoved the bare-breasted girl away to his right. At the same time there was a bright flash and a thunderous roar.

As the Kid reached for his holstered Schofield .44, he grimaced against the tooth-gnashing sting of the rock salt tearing into him.

CHAPTER 7
EL LEPROSO

The Kid groaned as he used his right hand to raise the Schofield. He looked toward the rear door to see the shadowy figure in high black boots, long gray duster, gray mask, and a low-crowned, black sombrero trimmed with silver stitching take one long step toward him, shifting the sawed-off shotgun in his hands slightly.

The Kid sucked back the pain of the salt wounds in his chest, shoulder, and neck, and cut loose with the Schofield, which leaped and roared in his hand. The bounty hunter known as the Leper jerked back slightly. The shotgun issued another blast of deafening thunder, flames jutting from the second barrel.

One of the Kid's slugs had hit its mark, however, and most of the rock salt hurled from the Leper's second barrel sprayed the fire, scattering ashes and half-burned branches. The Leper got his boots under him and dashed behind a large stone pillar on his right, about ten feet from the door.

The Kid's slugs chewed into the pillar, pluming rock dust and shards. When the Schofield's hammer clicked on an empty chamber, the Kid holstered it, grabbed his rifle from where he'd leaned it against the wall, and quickly jacked a fresh round into the breech.

He ran toward the half-naked girl lying on the floor near the fire and saw the Leper edge his shotgun out around one side of the pillar. The Kid fired the Winchester, jacked and fired two more times as he dove onto the girl, keeping her down and shielding her tender skin from a possible rock-salt blast.

The Kid lifted his head in time to see the Leper run out from behind the pillar toward the open door — a black-and-gray blur, the silver on the man's black sombrero flashing like starlight.

A jeering laugh rose like a scream.

The Kid's Winchester belched three more times, spitting orange flames and hot lead toward the bounty hunter. The Leper was too quick, however. The Kid's shots merely hammered the church walls around the door as the killer bounded out into the darkness from which he'd come, laughing.

"Stay here!" the Kid told the girl, and, as

the horses pitched and whinnied shrilly near the front of the church, he ran for the back door, punching cartridges through his Winchester's loading gate.

He bounded out the back door and stopped ten feet out from the church, aiming his Winchester from his right hip and whipping his gaze around, expecting a gun flash or the flicking of the Leper's jostling shadow.

Nothing.

Then a laugh sounded in the distance directly out from the church. The Kid wheeled to face it, saw the pale shapes of tombstones stretching away in the starry darkness, with here and there the large shadow of a shrine or an ancient crypt.

Out among those hunched figures, a gun flashed. A pistol popped. The bullet screeched past the Kid's left ear and spanged shrilly off the rear wall of the church behind him.

The Kid ran ahead and left and dove behind a near tombstone as the pistol flashed twice more, one slug tearing up gravel just inches behind the Kid's left boot. The other barked into the face of the stone behind which the Kid crouched.

The Kid shifted his rifle to his left hand — he'd become accustomed to shooting well with either — and edged his left eye and his Winchester around the gravestone's left side. He couldn't be sure in the darkness, but he thought a pale figure moved among the stones beyond him, about forty yards straight out from the church's back door.

Ka-chooo! Ka-chooo! Ka-choo — Ka-chooo!

The Winchester's reports echoed loudly off the church and caused the horses inside to whinny again shrilly.

The Leper's infuriating, mocking laugh rose again, this time from the Kid's right and maybe a little farther out from where the bounty hunter's gun had flashed.

"Kid, it's been a while!" he yelled in Spanish. "This works out well for me, *amigo.* I can bag two heads on one ride — yours and the girl's! *Amigo,* the General wants her *bad*!"

"Over my dead body!"

"That is very much my intention, my friend."

"He must want her alive," the Kid yelled, staring around the right side of his covering gravestone now, desperately trying to pick the bounty hunter out of the darkness. "Thus the rock salt!"

Despite the burning, bleeding wounds in his chest and shoulder, the Kid knew he'd been lucky so far. Usually, *El Leproso* didn't make such careless missteps as that which he'd made inside the church. The man's judgment had no doubt been clouded by Tomasina's heartrending beauty.

The Kid had no idea who the bounty hunter was behind that mask — if man he was and not a demon, as was surmised by the superstitious peons of northern Sonora. The Kid only knew that the bounty hunter known as *El Leproso* was as cold-blooded a killer as you'd likely ever find this side of the Sierra Madre.

And the man had been on the Kid's trail ever since the Kid had wreaked holy vengeance on the American cavalry soldiers who'd killed his Chiricahua Apache family and the Apache girl he'd intended to marry, and a two-thousand dollar bounty had been put on his head by President Grant himself — the very man the Kid had fought so nobly for in the Great Rebellion.

El Leproso called from the darkness: "The General wants his beloved very much alive, Kid! You see, he wants to give her to his men for a few magical nights in their bunkhouse and then watch them shoot her down like a hydrophobic dog in front of his garden wall!"

The Kid aimed at the place from which

the man's voice had come. The Winchester roared four times quickly, the slugs squealing through the darkness, screaming off rocks and ancient shrines.

The Kid hunkered down behind the marker, listening, waiting.

Silence closed over him, louder than before. His heartbeat quickened hopefully. Had one of his slugs taken down the bounty hunter?

As if in response to his silent query, a laugh rose — shrill and far away but as mocking as before.

"We'll meet again, soon, Kid!" called the Leper. "Please tell the girl she is most beautiful, even more lovely disrobed. But she must die just the same!"

Howling laughter.

Presently, hooves thudded. They dwindled quickly as *El Leproso* rode off in the night, and silence like a dark ocean tide washed in behind him.

A shadow flickered over the Kid's head. He jerked with a start, started to raise the Winchester. But it was only the ghost-faced owl lighting on a tombstone a few feet away — a small, gray apparition in the darkness, about the size of a dove.

The owl turned its pale face to him. Its

small eyes glowed as though from a fire within.

"You might've warned me a little earlier in there," the Kid grouched, canting his head toward the church.

The owl gave a sharp cry and flew away.

"Same to you," the Kid said.

CHAPTER 8
TAINTED WATER

Pancho Montoya stood on the brush-roofed gallery fronting his remote stage relay station, near the door he'd propped open with a rock to let some of the stove heat out. He'd finished serving menudo and tortillas to the small batch of passengers who'd just pulled in on the stage, and now the stocky, apron-clad station manager was about to enjoy a cigar.

To that end, Pancho started to scratch a lucifer to life on the clay *ojo* hanging from the rafters to his right, but stopped when something caught his eye. He scowled off across the desert directly east of the station.

The wicked desert wind had been blowing all day, kicking up sand and grit and tossing tumbleweeds this way and that. So it was difficult for Pancho Montoya to see who was approaching the station, the horse and its rider slowly taking shape amid the jostling veils of windblown sand.

Odd for a man to be riding in from that direction — across the desert as the hawk flies, where there were no trails except a few ancient Indio trails but mostly only *banditos*, renegade Yaqui, and rattlesnakes. Why not take the relatively well-maintained stage road that swept into the station from the north and continued on beyond it to the southwest?

But, then, earlier that day, two others had come from that same direction . . .

Holding his stove match in one hand in front of his chest, his cigar in the other hand, Montoya scowled into the barren, wind-whipped desert at the oncoming rider. Gradually, the station manager was able to see that the horse was a fine, coal-black Arabian. Its rider was a tall man in a gray duster that flapped in the ceaseless wind. He wore a thick lanyard across his chest, and the barrel of a rifle or shotgun jutted up from behind his right shoulder. He batted tall black boots against the horses' sides as he held the sleek mount at a steady lope. Moving as one, they swam up out of the storm like a murky mirage.

The stranger was a pale man wearing a bullet-crowned black sombrero, which was thonged tightly beneath the rider's chin to keep it from blowing off his head in this

304

maddening wind.

No, thought Montoya. Not a pale-faced man.

A man wearing a mask. Because of the wind, of course.

But then another thought occurred to Montoya as horse and rider continued to ride through the buffeting veils of blowing sand. As he continued to stare, riveted, at the gray-masked rider who was now within seventy yards and closing quickly, a dark apprehension nibbled at the edges of Montoya's consciousness.

The station manager crossed himself with the unlit cigar.

"Mierda," he whispered. *"Santos, por favor perdóname."* Saints, please spare me.

Montoya heard the horse's dull thuds as it entered the yard, its tall, masked rider checking it down to a trot. The stranger passed the stagecoach sitting before the station house, tongue drooping, awaiting the storm's end and a fresh team. He reined to a halt before Montoya, who winced at the knot of pulsating nerves at the back of his neck, hard as an oak knot.

"*Senor* Montoya," said *El Leproso* as he swung down from his silver-horned Spanish saddle complete with a garish, three-point breastplate, each of the points being a ham-

305

mered silver Spanish medallion. The Leper wrapped his reins over the hitch rack and looked up at Montoya, his dark eyes hard to read through the dusty flour-sack mask. "We meet again."

The eyes were red-rimmed. One sat slightly lower than the other, and, as Montoya had noted before, the left one tended to wander slightly. The Leper's lips were also red. Thick and red and oddly, irregularly shaped. And they smiled, showing the grimy, yellow teeth behind them.

The knot at the back of Montoya's neck grew tauter, but he suppressed a shudder of revulsion and turned his wince into a smile. "*El Leproso*, welcome!"

The Leper slipped his horse's fancy silver bit from its teeth, so it could draw water from the stock trough fronting the hitch rack, and then came up the gallery steps. He was a tall, lean man, and Montoya had to tilt his head back to look up at him.

The bounty hunter still wore that wet, red smile as he said, "Don't shit an old shitter, Pancho. Just tell me how long it's been since that half-breed and that redheaded girl passed through here."

Montoya's knees turned to putty. He stammered.

The Leper stared at him, canted his head

one way and then the other, waiting. Montoya looked at the two pistols holstered on the bounty hunter's hips, behind the duster, and the shotgun jutting up from behind his right shoulder.

He'd heard it was loaded with rock salt.

"You're gonna tell me now, or you're gonna tell me later," the Leper said softly, the burlap mask buffeting against his nose as he breathed, his flat, walleyed stare as menacing a thing as Montoya had ever seen. "But you're gonna tell me."

"Two hours."

"Headed where?"

"I thought I heard the girl mention San Gezo."

The bounty hunter frowned behind his mask. Then he nodded and his thick, misshapen lips shaped another grin. "I see," he said wistfully.

He turned to the clay *ojo* hanging from the rafters, beside Montoya. As he plucked the gourd dipper from the water pot and scooped up some water, he glanced at the station manager once more. "I don't care that you're not all that happy to see me, Pancho. I'm so damn happy to see you again, after all these months, *mi amigo,* that it makes up for the tenderness you so sorely lack with regards to my pretty ol' self."

Montoya wasn't sure what the bounty hunter had just said, and he didn't think it mattered. So much of what the killer said was mere nonsense that probably came from a man riding alone so much for most of his life. The station manager had heard that the man he knew only as *El Leproso* had contracted his hideous disease long ago, when he was very young.

For some reason, possibly because of some demon's curse on humanity, it hadn't yet killed him.

What Montoya was most concerned about now, however, was the precious water that the man had dippered up from the *ojo* and was holding about six inches from his disfigured face with its red lips rimed with dust.

El Leproso stared at Montoya as though reading the disgust in his mind. The bounty hunter swung the dipper out slightly, water sloshing onto the gallery's scarred wooden floor at his boots, and said, "Drink?"

Montoya smiled tensely and shook his head.

"You don't mind if I take a little, do you?"

Montoya looked down, the smile painted on his face, and shook his head though his guts writhed like snakes until he thought he would gag.

"Gracias, amigo."

The Leper drank loudly, slurping the water up through the hole in his mask, sounding like a dog. When he was through with one dipperful of the water, he scooped up some more and continued to drink loudly until he'd had his fill.

Then he dropped the dipper back down in the pot with a splash, and wiped his mouth with his dirty duster sleeve. He hitched his double cartridge belts and two black holsters on his hips. Each ornately tooled sheath contained a silver-chased, pearl-gripped Navy Colt .44. He adjusted his sombrero's chin thong as he dropped down the gallery steps and plucked his reins from the hitch rail.

When he'd swung up into the saddle, he pinched his dusty hat brim to the station manager.

"Till next time, Montoya . . . when I can stay longer and enjoy more of your delicious water."

He swung the sleek black Arabian around and rode away.

Hoof thuds died beneath the sighing wind.

Montoya turned his head slowly to the *ojo,* and grimaced.

Chapter 9
Shadows in the Wind

Atop a wind-battered ridge, the Rio Concho Kid stared through his brass-chased spyglass.

A ragged shadow moved out on the darkling plain.

Thunder rumbled. The Kid glanced at the sky. A vast, arrow-shaped cloud mass nearly as dark as night but with its belly laced with thin wisps of cottony white was edging toward him from the southwest, the same direction the wind was from. Again, thunder rumbled, causing the gravelly ground to vibrate. From the same direction, a vast shadow was sweeping across the land.

The Kid directed the spyglass once more to the northeast.

The gray shadow remained, flickering between curtains of windblown sand. The Kid lowered the spyglass, felt his jaws tighten.

That's right, El Leproso. You keep comin'.

310

I'd like nothin' better than to scour your ugly visage from my back trail once and for all!

How many years now, off and on, had the Leper been after him? Four? It felt like ten. He'd seen the man only a few times, mostly up north of the border.

The Kid glanced at the girl sitting a ways down the ridge behind him, the lower half of her face covered with a checked bandanna against the blowing dust. Her hair blew out behind her shoulders.

The air had cooled, and she wore a fringed elk-skin jacket, which, she said when she'd unwrapped it from her bedroll and donned it earlier, had belonged to her lover, Ernesto Alabando, a wandering *vaquero* who had ridden for a time for her father, before there were no longer any cattle to tend at *La Colina de Rosa*.

She yelled from behind her neckerchief and above the wind, "San Gezo is just over the next pass!"

"Still a half day's ride." The Kid shook his head. "We'll never make it before it rains and turns these arroyos to rivers!"

He looked down the ridge past Tomasina and their ground-reined horses to the abandoned goat herder's shack in the crease between this ridge and the next. "We'll spend the night here, finish our journey in

311

the morning." He offered a wan smile. "Don't worry, *senorita,* you'll be with your beau again soon."

She smiled with her eyes, crawled up to him, and rested her hand against his cheek. She held his gaze for a time, and again he felt the heat of the girl penetrating every cell in his body. At the same time, a dark cloud swept through him, for he knew that all the pent-up passion inside her was reserved for Ernesto Alabando.

She would do anything, even lie with another, compromise her purity, to see her lover again.

She lowered her hand from the Kid's face.

"He's out there, isn't he?" she asked, letting her gaze flick toward the eastern plain. *"El Leproso."*

"Yes."

"Will we be safe here?"

"As safe here as anywhere."

Thunder boomed violently, and the rain began to fall at a slant — heavy raindrops the size of silver dollars.

She smiled again, confidently. "You have a plan, don't you?"

He grinned devilishly. "Of course, I do, Tomasina." He climbed to his feet and took her hand. "Come on. Let's get inside before we have to swim for it!"

Hours later, when the rain had dwindled to a steady cadence on the stone shack's leaky brush roof, the Kid turned from where he'd been cleaning his guns at the stout wooden table.

He looked at Tomasina where she lay on the cot near the scorched stone fireplace. A fire danced and popped and smoked against the raindrops tumbling into it through the chimney. It cast a gentle glow upon the girl's right cheek and shone in the highlights in her hair.

She was even more beautiful in repose than she was awake. Asleep, she looked like a child. A sweet and tender, copper-haired, rose-lipped virginal child, eyelids pale as a dove's wings.

And then it wasn't Tomasina whom he was gazing at but his own life's one true love, the beautiful Apache princess Elina, whom he'd met when he'd returned to Arizona Territory after the war.

After rising to the rank of first lieutenant and witnessing so much killing, Johnny Navarro had yearned for the healing that he thought he could find only with his mother's people, the Chiricahua Apache, though his mother herself had died several years before from pneumonia. His father, Wayne Navarro, had been a rancher from the Great Bend country of Texas, and he'd disowned the Kid when the Kid had joined the Union army to fight against the Confederacy.

"Elina," the Kid whispered, reaching out to close his hand over the sleeping girl's shoulder. "Elina . . ."

She'd been killed by a drunken cavalry patrol — her and the rest of her small band, the People of the Ghost-faced Owl, when they'd been camped just north of the border in New Mexico Territory, in their traditional hunting grounds. The patrol had assumed they were the Apaches who'd been harassing the freight road between Lordsburg and Las Cruces, and they'd slipped into the canyon one night, set up their Gatling gun, and killed Elina and her entire band, while they'd slept in their wickiups.

The Kid had gone to Las Cruces with two braves for supplies. When they'd returned and the Kid saw the results of the massacre, he went as mad as a bruin fighting his way through a wildfire.

When the heavy clouds of insanity had parted, he'd stalked and killed every soldier in the patrol, some with the Gatling gun they'd used on the people who'd adopted him. He'd hacked out their eyes and cut out their hearts with his bowie knife, so that in the next world they would have no eyes to see with, no hearts to pump their blood with.

He'd left the killers' hearts and eyes for the coyotes and bobcats to fight over.

The ghosts of the killers would linger forever in the nether world, blind and hollow as scarecrows, wailing their eternal regrets for what they'd done to Johnny Navarro's people and Elina, his life's one true love . . .

And for two years following, he'd killed every soldier and lawman who came after him. Now it was mostly bounty hunters dogging his trail. He'd culled the herd until he was down now to the most dangerous stalkers — men like *El Leproso* . . .

His hand must have tightened on the girl's shoulder. She groaned, opened her eyes, turned to him. Her gaze shifted to something behind him. Her lower jaw sagged, and then the owl gave its raucous scream.

CHAPTER 10
TRICKERY BY STARLIGHT

The Rio Concho Kid swung around, his gun in his hand, clicking the Schofield's hammer back. The owl sitting on the ledge of the window behind him merely blinked its little eyes that reflected the crimson flames of the fire dancing in the hearth.

The Kid lifted the revolver's barrel, depressing the hammer.

"Does he follow you everywhere?" the girl asked.

"Pretty much."

The Kid rose and walked over to the table where his freshly cleaned and loaded Winchester lay.

Tomasina flung her blanket back and sat up, dropping her long legs over the edge of the cot. She was staring at the strange gray owl staring back at her from the window ledge.

"He's saying something . . . with his eyes. What?"

"He's telling me I need to keep my head clear. A real pain in the old caboose sometimes."

The Kid donned his hat and walked to the door.

"Is he out there?" Tomasina asked, her voice quavering slightly.

"That's what I'm gonna find out." He placed his hand on the leather-and-steel latch. "You stay here, keep your head down."

"Kid?"

He looked at her. She leaned forward, arms on her knees. "What was her name?"

He hesitated, turned to the door, felt a knot grow in his throat. "Elina," he said, and then opened the door and went out.

He took a moment to draw a deep breath, to suppress the clinging, gnawing grief and sorrow, the frustration of knowing that his life should have turned out so much differently from all this killing, all this lone wandering and running. He and Elina should be together. They should have a child, maybe another on the way.

They should have a small *rancho* along the Rio Concho, so many good years ahead . . .

He looked carefully around the old goat herder's shack, finding no boot prints but his own and the girl's in the clay mud. After he investigated the old lean-to stable and found both horses calm and undisturbed, he walked up the east ridge and hunkered down at the top.

About two hundred yards out on the dark eastern plain, a pinprick of yellow light danced in the velvety darkness. The Kid removed his spyglass from the pocket of his doeskin jacket, and, lying on his belly, propped on his elbows, he stared through the glass, adjusting the focus.

That he was staring at *El Leproso*'s camp and small cook fire there was little doubt. The man himself sat under a lean-to canopy, which he'd likely hastily erected for shelter against the storm. From this distance, even through the spyglass the Kid couldn't see much, but he made out a long shadow stretched out beside the flickering fire, leaning back against what appeared to be a saddle.

The shadow was capped with a black sombrero. Beneath the sombrero was the gray splotch of the bounty hunter's mask. As the Kid studied the camp, he watched the slender shadow of *El Leproso* rise, throw a stick on the flames and then pour a cup of coffee before sitting back down against his saddle and leisurely crossing his legs.

The Kid stared through the glass. His

heartbeat quickened.

El Leproso . . .

The old hunter took his time. He had patience. The Kid would give him that.

"What do you say we finish this, my old friend?" the Kid said under his breath, feeling his pulse throb in his temples. "Right now. Tonight."

He collapsed the telescope and returned it to his pocket. Rising, he picked up his Winchester, backed down the ridge a few yards and then turned and made his way along the slope toward the north.

He walked slowly and quietly, as he'd learned on his boyhood hunts with his Apache cousins along the Rio Bravo and the Rio Concho, which had given the Kid his nickname after he'd killed two US marshals along that tributary of the Rio Grande two years ago, when the lawmen had tried to arrest him and, failing that, tried to shoot him.

When he'd walked about six hundred feet north, he turned and headed east.

The Leper's fire flickered ahead and on his right though the Kid often lost sight of it, for he kept his head low, wending his way through pockets of wet brush and boulders, a flooded arroyo gurgling on his left.

He paused for a breather between two

large boulders. The owl's winged shadow fluttered over him, whistling softly through the chill, damp air, and lighted on a mesquite. The owl stared at its charge with its superior air, its umber eyes pulsating softly.

Annoyed, the Kid whispered, "Don't you have some pocket mice to hunt?"

The owl continued to stare at him obliquely.

The Kid sighed and continued walking, angling now almost directly toward the fire flickering ahead about fifty yards away but growing gradually larger as the Kid closed on it.

When he was forty yards from the fire, he hunkered down behind a boulder, and crouched there, still as stone, all his senses attuned. He did not look at the fire, for the light would compromise his night vision. He peered into the darkness around it, watching for movement, listening for sounds.

There was only the faint sighing of the wet earth and dripping plants, the yodeling of a distant coyote and the slight rasping of a burrowing creature somewhere off to the Kid's left — probably a kangaroo rat rebuilding its nest after the storm.

Very faintly he could hear the snapping of the Leper's fire. His keen nose did not tell him where the Leper's horse was tied, and that caused a fingernail of caution to rake the small of his back.

Usually, on a night as still as this, he could smell a horse from fifty yards away.

He could smell the fire and the coffee and beans that had been cooked over it, but not the horse.

The Kid squeezed the neck of his Winchester. He'd already levered a cartridge into the chamber. Now, pressing his tongue against his lower lip, he very slowly and quietly raked the hammer back with his right, gloved thumb. He sat with his back to the boulder between him and the fire.

Now he doffed his hat and turned his head to peer with his right eye around the side of the boulder. He could see only the low column of flames dancing beneath the tarpaulin erected atop two mesquite poles. The bounty hunter was likely on the other side of it, as he'd been before.

This was not a fair fight between honorable combatants. This was kill or be killed. The Kid would shoot *El Leproso* through the fire without warning.

He leaned hard to his right and gritted his teeth as he snaked the rifle along the right side of the boulder and pressed his cheek to the stock. He steadied the weapon and stared down the barrel, half closing one eye and mentally slowing his heartbeat and leeching every scrap of nervousness from his hands.

Now he could see the area beneath the tarpaulin clearly.

He blinked. His heart thudded.

Beyond the fire lay vacant ground.

His heart thudded again as the Kid rose slowly to his feet, continuing to aim over the Winchester's cocked hammer and down the barrel . . . at nothing but sand and gravel.

The saddle that *El Leproso* had been reclining against was gone.

His coffeepot and all the rest of his gear were gone.

No wonder the Kid hadn't smelled the man's horse.

He'd pulled out.

In the night's hushed silence, a girl's distant scream vaulted toward the stars.

Somewhere behind the Kid, the owl added its own bitter wail to that of the girl's.

To Tomasina's . . .

The Kid lowered the Winchester and ran.

CHAPTER 11
SAN GEZO

The Kid reined Antonia to a halt atop a hill and stared down the other side into the village of San Gezo.

It was a small collection of peasant shacks and stock pens circling a big, brown church. The church and its customary cemetery were the centerpiece of the village's central plaza, where a stone fountain stood, surrounded by craggy poplars.

The pale hills that surrounded the village were stippled with green, for the recent rains had nourished the local foliage. But it was not the foliage the Kid was interested in.

Since the first wash of dawn, he'd been following the tracks of a single shod horse. They'd led him here to the outskirts of San Gezo. The Kid knew why *El Leproso* hadn't killed Tomasina when he'd outfoxed the Kid the night before, and circled around and nabbed her.

The General wanted her alive, to torture

and kill her himself, or to watch his men kill her.

He likely wouldn't pay for a corpse.

But why had he brought her here and not directly to the General? Most likely, the Kid decided, he needed supplies and to rest his horse, for it was a three-day ride back to the General's *hacienda*. The night before, *El Leproso* hadn't taken the time to grab the girl's horse, so he'd need one of those, too, and the village was the best place around to find one.

But he wouldn't need the horse. Because the Kid had no intention of allowing the Leper to bring Tomasina back to the General for killing.

Carefully sweeping the morning-quiet village with his gaze, the Kid slid his Winchester out of its saddle boot, cocked it one-handed, and rested the barrel across his saddlebow. He brushed his right hand across the walnut-gripped Schofield holstered for the cross draw on his left hip, then nudged Antonia with his heels.

He started down the hill and into the outskirts of the village, where the humble stone, adobe, or tin-roofed plankboard shacks and stock pens crowded close along the trail.

Chickens pecked around some of the

shacks. A rooster crowed. Goats and pigs foraged. Somewhere on the other side of the village, in the pale hills to the southwest, a lone dog barked as though at something it had trapped under a gallery or in a privy.

The fresh morning breeze was touched with the aroma of breakfast fires and the winey fragrance of rose blossoms.

As the Kid continued toward the square, he saw a few people moving about their yards. A boy in peasant pajamas was hauling a wooden bucket of water from a flooded wash. When the boy saw the tall, grim stranger on the blaze-faced sorrel, his eyes widened under a mussed wing of short, black hair, and the boy hurried toward a tumbledown shack on the right side of the street.

He went inside and turned a frightened stare on the Kid as he closed the sagging plank door behind him.

The Kid slowed Antonia down more and, squeezing the neck of his Winchester, followed a slight bend in the street.

On the far side of the bend lay the plaza and the church ahead and on the right, a row of pale adobe shops and a wooden barn with adjoining blacksmith shop on the left. An old man in a straw sombrero sat on a bench outside one of the shops.

He was long-faced and reed thin. His skinny legs were crossed, his feet bare. He was smoking a cigarette. As he watched the Kid without expression, he shook his head once and crossed himself.

At the same time, the Kid heard a gurgling, groaning sobbing. He swept the square with his gaze, the hair under his shirt collar prickling almost painfully.

Then he saw Tomasina.

She stood in front of the church's stout wooden doors, partly concealed by the morning's cool, blue shadows. She was not alone, for she was standing on the shoulders of an old, gray man in a brown clerical robe and rope-soled sandals. The old *padre* was groaning and sighing, shifting his weight from one foot to the other as he balanced the girl on his shoulders, his gnarled hands wrapped around her ankles.

Tomasina sobbed as she looked toward the Kid, whose heart turned a cold somersault in his chest when he saw the noose around the girl's neck. The rope trailed up from the noose to the bell tower where it was tied to the large, cast-iron bell's clapper.

The rope was nearly taut. If the *padre* dropped her, she'd hang. She'd suffocate if her neck didn't snap first.

The Kid swung his right boot over his saddle horn, dropped straight down to the ground and, holding the Winchester in one hand, took two lunging steps toward the *padre* and the girl.

"Kid, no!" she screamed.

The echo of her yell hadn't died before one dust plume rose mere inches in front of the Kid. The crack of a rifle flatted out over the village, echoing dully.

The Kid's boots lifted more dust as he skidded to a stop, slinging his arms out for balance and jerking his gaze to his left, the direction from which the lead had been slung.

The Leper was on one knee in front of the stable, aiming a sixteen-shot Henry rifle with a brass receiver against his shoulder. Gray smoke curled from the barrel.

The Leper's double-barreled shotgun poked up from behind his right shoulder.

The lips behind the mask were spread in a delighted grin as *El Leproso* ejected a spent shell and pumped a fresh one into the chamber.

CHAPTER 12
BOOT HILL SHOOT-OUT

The Leper canted his masked head toward the girl and the *padre.* "A wretched way to die — hanging."

The old *padre* continued to grimace and groan, shifting his weight to balance the girl on his shoulders.

"Let me go, *Padre,*" Tomasina said. "I'm dead, anyway."

"Never, my child!" the old, gray-bearded man said, though the Kid could see that his knees were buckling and he was beginning to stoop forward beneath his burden. The girl probably didn't weigh much over a hundred pounds, but even that was too much weight for his ancient, spindly frame.

"Let me cut her down, damn you," the Kid snarled.

The Leper straightened slowly, lowering his Henry slightly but keeping it cocked and ready. "Over my dead body."

He sidestepped away from the stable,

heading toward the fountain and the cotton-woods that stood between the stable and the church. The burlap mask buffeted against his contorted face as he breathed.

Rage seared through the Kid's veins like acid. All the years he'd been trying to stay ahead of this man only to confront him now, with the girl's life in the balance. Once the Leper was dead, both the Kid and the girl would be free . . . if the Kid could kill him fast enough, before the old *padre*'s back gave out.

The trouble was, the Kid was well aware that *El Leproso* was his most formidable foe. What else did the man have except his ability to maim, torture, and kill?

"That can be arranged!" The Kid took one running step forward and threw himself to the ground, clicking his Winchester's hammer back and firing.

The Leper laughed and stepped to his right as the Kid's bullet plunked into the cottonwood behind him. The Leper aimed his Henry from his right hip and fired three fast rounds, smoke and flames stabbing toward the Kid, who rolled to his left as each bullet blew up dust just inches to his right.

The Kid rolled onto his belly, jerked his Winchester up and fired his own three rounds quickly, watching in frustration as *El Leproso* dove behind the fountain. When the Kid's reports had stopped echoing, he could hear the bounty hunter laughing, taunting him.

"It is all right, *Padre,*" Tomasina was saying in a gentle voice as she gazed sympathetically down at the old brown-robe, who was grunting and wheezing shrilly through gritted teeth as his shoulders continued to slump beneath the girl's weight. "Please . . . just let me go, *Padre.* Drop to your knees!"

"Never!"

The Kid glanced at the fountain. He couldn't see the Leper crouched behind it though he could hear the killer's hysterical laughter.

"Tomasina, look down!" the Kid shouted as he swung toward her, gaining a knee.

Pumping a fresh round into the Winchester's chamber, he slammed the stock against his shoulder and lined up his sites on the rope above the girl's head. He drew his index finger back against the Winchester's trigger.

At the same time that his own gun belched, he felt a searing burn in his upper left arm. The blast of the Leper's own rifle reached his ears as he watched his slug carve a dimple out of the church wall just a hair right of the taut rope above Tomasina's head.

The bullet burn across the Kid's arm punched him backward. He dropped his rifle and threw his right arm out to steady himself. At the same time, *El Leproso* stepped out to the right of the fountain and walked along it toward the Kid, aiming his rifle straight out from his right hip.

Smoke and flames lapped from the barrel. The Kid sucked a sharp breath as the bullet carved a burning line across the nub of his right cheek and across his right ear before thumping into the street behind him.

El Leproso threw his head back and laughed. "Look at it this way, Kid, your running days are over. Now you can join that Apache whore you were so fond of. I heard the soldiers really had fun with her . . . really made her *howl like a whore* . . . before they cut her to ribbons with their Gatling gun!"

Fury a raging puma in the Kid's heart, he rolled sideways as *El Leproso* drilled another round at him. The Kid palmed his Schofield and leaped to his feet, firing once as the Leper threw himself behind a cottonwood. The Kid fired again, tearing bark from the tree, and then wheeled and sprinted toward the church.

Laughing wildly, *El Leproso* sent three

rounds buzzing like enraged hornets around the Kid's head.

All three slugs slammed into the side of the adobe hovel beside the church a half second before the Kid bounded into the break between the *casa* and the church. He continued running, sprinting hard down the shady, trash-strewn gap. He dashed around the corner and pressed his back to the church's rear wall, breathing hard, gritting his teeth against his fury and the hot burn in his arm and across his cheek and ear.

He looked around.

To his right hunched the *casa* and a stable flanking it. Inside the *casa,* a baby was crying. To the Kid's left, beyond the church, lay open ground rolling off toward the pale, cactus-stippled hills. Straight out behind the church was a small cemetery adorned with shrines.

Quickly, the Kid tripped the catch and broke the Schofield open to expose the cylinder. He plucked out his spent cartridges, tossing them into the dirt at his boots, and replaced them with fresh from his shell belt. He snapped the gun closed, spun the cylinder, and pressed his back harder against the church's cool wall, pricking his ears to listen for *El Leproso.*

The man was coming.

But from which side of the church?

He got his answer a second later.

El Leproso stepped quickly around the corner to the Kid's left, aiming his Henry along the rear wall from his shoulder. The rifle's black maw appeared to open like a lion's jaws.

As the rifle thundered, the Kid lurched straight out away from the wall, dove over a tombstone, rolled off a shoulder and came up shooting.

Bam! Bam!

He glimpsed *El Leproso* jerking back behind the corner of the church as the Kid's bullets chewed adobe from the wall where the hunter had been standing a half second before.

The Kid heaved himself to his feet, ran back across the graveyard, and lofted himself into the air as the Leper's rifle barked twice more, one slug nudging the Kid's left heel as he careened over another stone and slammed into the ground behind it.

The Kid twisted around, squatted on his heels.

Stretching his Schofield over the gravestone, he saw *El Leproso* dashing toward him, crouching, holding his rifle low across his belly in both hands, the shotgun jutting from behind his right shoulder.

The Kid fired two shots. One slug kissed the nap of the man's gray duster sleeve; the second slug blew the Leper's sombrero down his back, where it hung by its thong.

Fleet as a puma, *El Leproso* dove to his left behind a shrine bright with fresh flowers and bordered by a rusted wrought-iron fence.

The crazy killer's hysterical laughter rose from behind the shrine, vaulting over the pale stones toward the lightening morning sky.

"I think you're too late, Kid!" the bounty hunter squealed. "I think I just heard that old fool's knees pop. Oh, well — there's an even bigger bounty on you!"

He edged his hatless, burlap-wrapped head around the side of the shrine.

The Kid held his breath though his heart was leaping wildly in his chest, and fired the Schofield.

His slug tore into the shrine's tall upright stone.

As *El Leproso* snaked his Henry around the side of the shrine, the Kid ducked behind his own covering gravestone. In the corner of his eye, the words carved into the stone caught his fleeting attention, and he knew a moment's vague befuddlement.

Ernesto Alabando.

Tomasina's one true love.

The Leper's slug loudly hammered the stone, cleaving it in two along a hair-thin fault line.

Both sides slumped away, leaving the Kid exposed.

He bounded off his knees, ran crouching to his right, wanting to save the last cartridge in his six-shooter because he'd never get a chance to reload. A thundering blast much louder than a rifle report rose from the direction of the shrine. The Kid knew immediately that what he'd heard was the Leper's double-barreled shotgun being brought into play.

The squash-sized fist of rock salt blew up a dogget of earth and nudged the Kid's left boot into the other one. The Kid left his feet. When he came down, his head glanced off another tombstone as he slammed onto his right shoulder and lay with his foot stinging now as badly as his cheek and his ear.

He felt as though a rail spike had been driven through his right temple. Warm blood trickled down that side of his face. He lay on his back, arms and legs akimbo, his vision flickering as the ground rolled like ocean swells around him.

In the back of his head a voice was screaming, *"Tomasina!"*

"I'm not gonna kill you, Kid!" the Leper shouted. The Kid heard his footsteps growing louder as the stalker walked toward him. "Gonna make you hurt *bad*. Have *fun* killin' you *slow!*"

The Leper laughed.

The Kid suppressed his misery, gathering himself.

Bunching his lips and hardening his jaws, he rolled onto his left shoulder and extended the cocked Schofield toward *El Leproso,* who just then stopped and grinned behind his mask as he aimed his double-barreled shotgun at the Kid's face.

At the same time, a raucous screech rose on the Kid's right — a sound like an entire flock of eagles in an ear-rending dustup over a dead rattlesnake.

The bounty hunter jerked slightly with a start and the rock salt fired from the roaring shotgun blew up rocks and dust a good foot ahead and left of the Kid's extended revolver.

The Kid triggered the Schofield, watched his slug drill a quarter-sized hole in the Leper's dusty mask, through the dead center of *El Leproso*'s forehead. The man's head jerked violently back. Then it straightened on his shoulders, wobbling slightly.

The Leper opened his gloved hands, and the smoking shotgun fell slack against his chest, dangling by its lanyard.

El Leproso stood staring at the Rio Concho Kid. Slowly, the smile left his thick, red lips behind the mask, which grew red quickly as the killer's blood ran down the inside of it. The Leper's eyes rolled back into his head until only their whites were visible through the holes cut in the cloth.

El Leproso fell straight back atop a grave, kicking up tan dust painted gold by the morning sunlight. He lay there as though he'd been dropped from the sky.

The Kid glanced at the owl perched atop a tombstone about fifty feet away. Smugly, the bird was preening under a half-raised wing.

Tomasina . . .

The Kid climbed heavily to his feet, dropped his empty pistol, leaped the dead Leper's body, and sprinted along the side of the church toward the front. He dashed around the corner, and stopped, raking air in and out of his chest.

A cold stone dropped in his belly.

The *padre* was on his hands and knees, bawling, his tears dribbling into the dirt beneath him.

Tomasina hung by the rope around her

neck, twisting slowly from side to side.

The Kid screamed her name, and, sliding his bowie knife from his belt sheath, sprinted over to her, leaped into the air. He swiped the knife across the rope once before gravity drove him to the ground.

"Tomasina!" he cried, desperately bounding off his heels once more, slashing at the rope above the girl's head until the last strand broke.

The Kid dropped the knife. The girl fell into his arms.

He collapsed to his knees, holding the girl's slack body across them. Her cheeks were pale, her eyes closed.

"Tomasina," the Kid cried, shaking her, feeling tears mingle with the blood on his cheek.

Her chest moved. Her lips fluttered. She drew a breath, and her eyes opened.

The Kid stared down at her, his lower jaw hanging in shock.

"I . . . I came here to join Ernesto . . . in the cemetery," she rasped out barely audibly. She stared up into the Kid's relieved eyes. "He is there, where *El Leproso* put him."

"Ah, Tomasina," the Kid said.

"I came to join him . . . because I thought life was only big enough for one love. For only *one true love.*"

She smiled, lifted her arms weakly, wrapped them around his neck. "But now I know that's not true, Kid."

"Me, too, Tomasina," the Kid said, laughing with exhilaration. "Me, too!"

The Rio Concho Kid lowered his head to Tomasina's, pressed his lips to her ripe mouth, and kissed her long and tenderly.

The Rio Concho Kid and Tomasina De La Cruz will return . . .

ABOUT THE AUTHOR

Peter Brandvold has penned over seventy fast-action westerns under his own name and his pen name, Frank Leslie. He is the author of the ever-popular .45-Caliber books featuring Cuno Massey as well as the Lou Prophet and Yakima Henry novels. Head honcho at "Mean Pete Publishing," publisher of harrowing western ebooks, he lives in Colorado. Visit his website at www .peterbrandvold.com. Follow his blog at: www.peterbrandvold.blogspot.com.

The employees of Thorndike Press hope you have enjoyed this Large Print book. All our Thorndike, Wheeler, and Kennebec Large Print titles are designed for easy reading, and all our books are made to last. Other Thorndike Press Large Print books are available at your library, through selected bookstores, or directly from us.

For information about titles, please call:
(800) 223-1244

or visit our Web site at:
http://gale.cengage.com/thorndike

To share your comments, please write:
Publisher
Thorndike Press
10 Water St., Suite 310
Waterville, ME 04901